HANNAH R. GOODMAN

TILL IT STOPS BEATING

Black Rose Writing | Texas

The final approval for this literary material is granted by the author.

First printing

This is a work of fiction. Names, characters, businesses, places, events and incidents are either the products of the author's imagination or used in a fictitious manner. Any resemblance to actual persons, living or dead, or actual events is purely coincidental.

ISBN: 978-1-68433-080-5
PUBLISHED BY BLACK ROSE WRITING
www.blackrosewriting.com

Printed in the United States of America
Suggested Retail Price (SRP) $18.95

Till It Stops Beating is printed in Chaparral Pro

ACKNOWLEDGMENTS

I would like to thank the following people for their time and support: my sisters-in-writing authors Kacey Vanderkarr, Kristen Tsetsi, and Heather Christie; my sista-from-anotha-mista and BFF Alyssa; my older daughter, Chelsea, for being the best editor a mom (or writer) could ask for; my younger daughter, Vivian, for her words (and hugs) of encouragement; my husband, Mike, for his patience all of these years (decades) as I chased my dream; my mother Sheryl, father Louis, and, sister Jen, for providing me with endless good copy from my childhood; my mentor and friend, David Yoo, for his infinite support and belief in me as a writer; and, finally, my cat, Zoe, for being the purrfect distraction as I edited this book.

Though this book was birthed long ago, its (deep) revisions were more recent, and I have to thank not only those above for their assistance with that, but also two important readers, Allie Gilles and Christina Irace.

I dedicate this book to my own "Bubbie" a.k.a. my grandmother Bernice, who inspired me to chase this writing dream.

TILL IT STOPS BEATING

PART 1
SENIOR YEAR

CHAPTER ONE
JELLY DOUGHNUTS

September 15th

Three weeks ago, today... we were kissing underneath the giant oak tree in my back yard... five months and four days ago we were in my car, holding hands, reminiscing about sophomore year when we were together...One year and nine months ago we were breaking up on my front lawn—

"Friends, seniors, texters..." Mrs. Dubois plops two boxes of doughnuts onto her desk.

I slam my journal shut while the rest of the class shoves their phones in their pockets.

"...lend me your ears..."

Leaning on my hand, visions of Justin, his blue-grey eyes...and chocolate doughnuts dance in my head...

"I come not to burden you but to help you..." Mrs. Dubois puts her hands together.

"...with your college application essay."

Everyone groans while I mumble, to no one in particular, "Chocolate glazed?" Because if I can't be left alone to daydream and write about Justin, I better get a chocolate glazed.

"Thou doth protest too much!" She snatches both boxes and clutches them to her slender body, "Shut thy traps or lose thy doughnuts!"

The class stifles further moans. No one wants to sabotage Doughnut Day, the highlight of AP English so far, this year—aside from the soliloquies performed by Lady Dubois.

The Lady opens the boxes, revealing a cornucopia of sugar-dusted and glazed delights. "One doughnut each!" she bellows. "In return, I want a one-page, rough draft of your personal statement."

The entire class bustles up to her desk, barking at each other over who gets the chocolate glazed. I don't bother to follow. With eighteen other seventeen-year-olds to compete with, my chances of snagging the very best doughnut flavor are not even slim, they're just none. Kind of like my chances of having a relationship with Justin again. None.

So, I bend my head and scribble "My Personal Statement" and chew my pen cap while my fellow classmates settle into their seats and munch on sticky doughnuts, only mildly better for you than a pen cap, but certainly tastier. I scratch out:

~~My Personal Statement~~

Because I hear thy muse, and she speaks in my mind:

Ode to the Asshole Who Broke My Heart

But he's not an asshole anymore, so that's not right.

Ode to The Former Asshole Who Broke My Heart

Better.

Ode to The Boy Who Continues to Break My Heart But Probably Doesn't Mean to

Yes! The muse continues to sing inside my head, inspiration coming in the form of Lady Dubois's doughnuts:

No doughnut or pastry can distract me.

I think of Him, continuously.

Why oh why can't I stop this miserable shit— that makes me write this horrible bit?

A reformed bad boy
Who's been at Military school
Returning home occasionally
Each time making me a fool
No text or phone call in between
I know it's not because he's mean.
My true love finally has stopped his shitty ways
So why oh why can't we be together even if it's not every day?

All I do is replay that kiss unable to let go of Him that I miss
I am clearly hexed—
'cause all I do is write crappy shit poetry and think about my ex.

The muse stops singing, so I look up ...and see a friggin' *jelly* doughnut in front of me. I shoot a glare at my best guy friend Peter, whose busy stuffing—you guessed it—a chocolate glazed into his mouth. "That's for bailing on us this weekend," he says, his mouth full of chocolate.

"Does the punishment really fit the crime?" I ask, wrinkling my nose at the jelly mess in front of me.

"Yes." He downs the rest of the doughnut in one bite.

"I'll make up for it after school!" My other best friend Susan leans over my shoulder, her short, blonde hair brushing my face as she plants a kiss on my cheek. "Chocolate chip cookies. With organic chips!"

I turn and give Susan a weak smile then stare back at the hole-less pastry ...aha!...The muse, she sings again...of the repulsive doughnut! "Thank you, Peter!" I say, and he gives me a weird look then shrugs, and I dip my head down again and write:

Jelly doughnuts don't fit the part
And there is a huge whole in my stupid, broken heart

Peter leans across the aisle to my desk, his floppy brown hair falling over his eyes. "Thank me for what?"

"Nothing—" I say, closing my notebook. If he knew I was writing another Ode To That Whom We Do Not Speak Of...

"Wanna bite?" Susan, says thrusting a vanilla cruller at me, her signature bright pink lipstick lining the bitten into doughnut.

I wrinkle my nose at her. "You're not mad at me?"

"No. But, you do have to set a time limit to this whole feeling sorry for yourself thing." And before I can protest, she sticks out a gloppy, doughnut-covered tongue at me and when I roll my eyes, she adds, "You don't know what you're missing, Hickman."

"I'm not feeling sorry for myself!" I say and play with the loose paper dangling out of my spiral-bound notebook.

"Sure, you're not. I'll take that off your hands." Peter nods to the doughnut in front of me.

I push the jelly mess towards him.

Lady Dubois booms from behind her desk. "Back to work! Isn't that your second doughnut, Mr. Shaw?"

Peter hangs his head in ass-kissing shame. "Yes, M'lady! Sorry!" Once Lady Dubois moves on to her next victim, he dives into doughnut number two.

Jelly plops out onto his napkin and my hand flies over my mouth.

Gross.

I vaguely hear Mrs. Dubois say something to the kid at her desk about "safeties" and "reaches," a.k.a. That Which I Have No Interest In. Not safety nor reach or anything in between.

I go back to my journal, far more useful to me right now than a personal statement.

Justin and I can't happen. I've gone over this a thousand times. I glance at Peter licking his fingers and then back at Susan, but just get the top of her blonde head as she furiously writes in her curly handwriting. A shadow darkens over my desk. I have no idea how long she's been there, but suddenly Lady Dubois is standing next to me saying:

"A college essay in verse can certainly give you that extra boost in the eyes of admissions officers."

That doughnut I didn't eat seems to be stuck in my throat.

She has my notebook in her hands and is scanning the page. I open my mouth, but only a weird croak comes out and, whoops! The bell rings.

Lady sighs and hands me back my notebook. "Keep at it. And don't forget, end it with a sense of hope. Colleges like that." My face burning, I nod, shove my notebook into my bag, and dart out with Peter and Susan trailing behind me. A sense of hope? Then the only thing that poem is good for is "my stupid broken heart."

·　　·　　·　　·　　·

After school, I'm sunk deep into Susan's plush couch in her TV room, holding a plate of fragrant chocolate chip cookies. Baked in honor of me because of the jelly doughnut fiasco last period.

"The scent of chocolate helps depression," Dr. Susan tells me from where she is perched on the arm of an oversized, orange chair.

My ears perk up. Susan and Peter nod at me and the plate of goodies, so I take a giant inhale... and promptly begin to cough. This makes them crack up until my cough turns into a fit, that's when Susan leaps up and starts whacking me on the back while Peter starts screaming about the Heimlich maneuver.

"Guys! Stop! I'm fine."

They both freeze and mumble, "Jesus you scared us" and "Just looking out for you." Then squish themselves back into the chair, together this time. Attached at the hip is putting it mildly. Attached at the shoulder, thigh, hip, knee.

After a few moments of silence where we all catch our breath, Peter offers, "Chocolate also releases the same endorphins as making out."

This makes the two of them giggle like seventh graders, while all I can think of with the words make out is—

"Justin." Oh, no. I said his name out loud.

"Ha! I told you so!" Peter shouts and leaps up, bumping Susan off the chair.

She crashes to the floor. "Hey!"

"Sorry." He points a finger at me. "But I knew it! And your essay was about That Who We Aren't Supposed to Speak Of."

"It was a poem." I correct him not even attempting to deny it. Why bother. These two know me better than I know myself.

Susan stands up, her nose ring gleaming in the florescent basement light. She gives him a light push. "Leave her alone, Petey. Of course, she's still recovering from the Return and Departure of Lover Boy." She walks over and rubs my head. "It's okay." She takes a cookie and crashes next to me. I clutch the plate as the remaining cookies bounce.

Peter crosses his arms. "Maybe she needs to actually try and get over you-know-who."

Susan smirks at him. "Cause you're an expert on Getting Over Him? Um, wait...aren't you in your first serious relationship?"

"What about Tim?" Peter hugs his arms tightly around himself.

We all take a long moment of silence: Tim was a closeted piece-of-shit-jock who hooked up with Peter on the down-low and when there was an inkling it might get out, Football Hero Tim beat the shit out of our Peter.

"That was not a relationship. That was a disaster." By the tone of her voice, Susan is clearly trying to lighten the mood.

"True." Peter uncrosses his arms. "Anyway, karma is a bigger bitch than any of us—now he's at some homophobic, religious school."

"Oh, snap!" Susan reaches out to high-five Peter who then high fives me.

Mood lightened.

"Hold on." Peter adds to Susan. "What about us?"

"Us?" Susan raises an eyebrow. "Honey, in case you forgot, you dumped me and then you came out. You're one boy I couldn't have and then two is The Total-Package, Shamus."

We all shake our heads.

Back in the spring, just days before they were supposed to get matching tattoos, Susan caught The Total Package kissing an ex-girlfriend who had the very same tattoo that Susan was supposed to get. The "yin" symbol to his "yang."

She continues, "So that makes me the expert in Boys You Want But Can't Be With. Not you."

"Amen!" I declare and thrust a piece of cookie under my nose, happy that my stupid broken heart is out of the spotlight.

Peter snatches the cookie and the plate from me. "Enough with sniffing the friggin' cookies. You're gonna inhale one up your nose and then we're going to have to do the Heimlich for real." He puts the plate on the coffee table.

"To my nose?" I cock my head at him.

"You know what I mean."

"Why am I getting the abuse?" I frown.

"Sorry," Peter says and clasps his hands together. "I just want you to be happy. Trying some tough love...and failing." He plops down next to me and throws an arm around my shoulders.

"I say we take a break from all of this sad sack shit," Susan reaches for the remote. "Let's get our Dawson on. It will make you feel better, Maddie."

Click. On screen Joey—with her annoying, puppy-dog-pained expression—explains to Dawson why she kissed Pacey, even though she was supposed to now be with Dawson (and not Pacey).

Finger wagging at the TV, I say, "This stupid love triangle goes on for the entire Dawson series..."

"And it never gets old," Susan throws a knowing glance at me.

"But these characters actually never change," I protest. "Subtract the love triangle but add Boy I Can't Get Over, and Welcome to Maddie's Creek."

"Shhhh," Peter whispers, squeezing my shoulder with his eyes still on the screen.

I lean into Peter and watch Dawson and Joey cry on the screen now. Most boys I know don't cry, yet another reason this show annoys me...on top of the fact that Dawson and Joey never seem to get over their teeny bop love, even when they're practically adults...Justin and I were together when we were freshmen and sophomores...I'm a senior for god sake, and he doesn't even go to school here, and I'm still busy waiting and pining...hanging on to one stupid make out session...

How does Dawson eventually get over Joey? He dates another girl...My god what have I been doing for the past year and nine months? Not going out with guys...at least ones I like...of which there has been two, at most.

Which makes me realize something.

"Guys!"

"Shhh!" Susan says. "This is the best part—" Susan mouths along with Dawson, "All that matters right now is what you want."

"F- Dawson and his stupid creek! I'm having an epiphany!"

"Can you just wait, like, two minutes?" Susan says.

"No!" I reach for the remote.

"Hells-to-the-no!" Susan snatches it back.

Peter and Susan (together as Dawson) recite, "You want him like I want you. You love him like I love you. Only the difference is, he loves you back the same way."

A tear falls from Susan's face. Peter sucks his breath in.

"Are you guys kidding me?"

Peter turns away from the TV. "I just can't watch the rest."

"Good!" I pluck the remote from Susan's hand. "'Cause it's time for Maddie's Creek, okay?"

Neither of them protests. I click off the TV.

I stand and face them, pointing a finger. "Listen to me: I can't keep doing the same thing—" I think so fast I almost miss it. "I'm gonna go out with a boy. Not just any boy, either. Someone I like."

"Really?" they ask together. "Today?"

"Soon."

"Okayyyy," they say, slowly, I practically see the radar signals between them. "Who?"

"I don't know." That cute guy who sits in front of me in Physics? Or maybe the other editor of the literary magazine, with the puppy eyes? Why can't I remember anyone's name?

"We'll help you!" Peter says.

"Yes...mmmm." I pace back and forth in front of them. "No. The one time I let you do that..."

"Oh, come on. Roy was sweet." Susan pipes in.

I stop pacing and shake my head. "His breath smelled of moth balls and...he farted on the date. I mean, come on."

"Valid point." Peter taps his chin. "How about Charlie?"

I make a who's-that face.

"Come on, Maddie." Susan reaches out and tugs at my arm. "Adorable Physics Charlie who always asks you for your mechanical pencil?"

"Maybe." That's his name!

I squat in front of them and they lean in close as I tell them, "Most of all...I'm gonna stop writing bad poetry about Justin...and stop replaying the make out session we had." Our hands and mouths roaming all over each other, telling me that he still loved me.

They look at me funny but then burst into applause, and I leap up and take a bow, as Susan says with a smile, "You know, I think this year Maddie's Creek is going to be a whole lot more interesting than Dawson's!"

CHAPTER TWO
GOIN' BACK TO CALI...I DON'T THINK SO.

September 18

There goes my promise to stop obsessing over J. Just finished watching *The Princess Bride* and BAM! I'm back in time...Whenever *The Princess Bride* was on TV, J would call me. This began way before we were dating, back when we were just kids, back when it was just the four of us, me, Justin, Susan, and Peter...The Jew Crew (even though some of us were halfies). He would call me and then we would sit on the phone and watch it together, saying the lines:

> **Me/Buttercup:** Farm boy, polish my horse's saddle. I want to see my face shining in it by morning.
> **J/Westley:** As you wish...*you silly wench*
> **Me/Buttercup** Farm boy, fill these with water—please.
> **J/Westley** As you wish. *Please my ass.*
> **Me/Buttercup:** Farm boy... fetch me that pitcher.
> **J/Westley:** As you wish. ...*Where's my please?*

He would ad-lib. I, of course, always stuck to the script.
CUZ THAT'S WHAT MADDIE DOES.

Then when Buttercup and Westley would be making out, we would get all quiet. Sometimes Justin would say stuff like *how come girls say one thing but mean the opposite?* Or I would offer, *of course they're making out...Girls always like boys they aren't supposed to be with.*

How prophetic...

October 4

Why do I still want him? Why do I still think about him? Why can't I let go? I don't even really know him anymore. Yeah, we had a random make out session in my back yard when he came home at the end of the summer. Yes, clothes almost came off. Yes, I wanted them to all come off.

I'm so sick of myself.

October 15

I think I have to do what my Bubbie always says she does when she's down...

Act as if...

Act *as if* I'm happy.

I'm not sure if that's what she means, actually.

But I'm sick of myself so...I'm gonna act as if.

Friday, November 8th

I got a new laptop. Dad bought it for me at the Apple store in town. "A pre-college gift," he said. "Something to make senior project and applying to college a little easier." Then he winked. He's so obvious. I know what he's trying to do. He knows I haven't opened one of those college guidebooks he bought me.

We had just finished a run outside and were freezing, so we went to get coffee at Starbuck's. He turned a relaxing Sunday morning into an opportunity to give me his favorite mini lecture about how important college is: "Socially, Madeline, socially this is crucial. You will meet all kinds of people, and you and I both know that you won't get that staying here in Lincoln." Other lectures of note have been the: Education Is The Ticket To Success, and Knowledge Is Power.

I've rewritten my college essay five times, and no it's not in verse as Mrs. Dubois suggested. I'm signed up to take the SATs for a second time. But only because this is what I'm supposed to do and what everyone else is doing.

As if.

My cell phone vibrates, dancing down the table toward my empty cup of coffee. My usual English Breakfast tea just doesn't do it for me like a sugar-infused, extra-foam latte. My heart pounds at the thought of all that yummy sugar and caffeine. Gotta cut down. I take a breath to calm my heart. Gotta cut down.

The phone teeters on the edge of the table. I just stare at it. Then it vibrates a last time and tumbles into my bag under the table. "Good," I say out loud and flex my fingers over the table. "Time to tackle chapter 1 of my senior project." Yeah, right, I think. I'd rather read my pathetic journal entries. "Way to go, Maddie," I say.

"Did you say something?" The hipster guy next to me pulls out his ear buds and asks.

"Just talking crazy to myself!" I say, all chipper. As if.

"Cool." He nods and sticks his ear buds back in.

"How is that possibly cool?" I whisper to my empty coffee cup. I am talking crazy to myself. Time to end my journal obsessing and get to work.

I close the red, cloth-covered notebook and push it to the side, then slap down my notebook filled with my senior project stuff. Thumbing through it for inspiration, I lean on my elbow and read from the first page of the summary of my yet-to-be-titled book:

Mya is heartbroken after both her boyfriend and sister fall off the deep end because of drinking and drugs...

Totally borrowed from my life.

Determined to get closure, Mya travels across the country to the boyfriend who is in rehab. On the way, she meets a group of Jesus types who take her into their compound for a few days and try to convert her to Christianity... until she starts chanting her haftarah from her bat mitzvah. It works like garlic to vampires and they show her the door.

Although heavily influenced by Lifetime's *Deprogramming Amy*, (about, you guessed it, a heartbroken high school girl who runs off with a cult), it's not quite the same. Poor Amy in the movie was forced to dress like an Amish person and make out with one of the old dudes in the cult. Bummer.

Mya flashes her Star of David a few times at the Jesus freaks, which results in one of them yanking it off her neck just as she escapes.

Mrs. Dubois wrote in the margin, in bold green letters, "reconsider the cult aspect."

She escapes and makes her way to boyfriend Dylan's rehab where, after a series of obstacles mainly in the form of a nasty front desk clerk and security guard, she steals into Dylan's room and pours her heart out.

Blank pages follow. Pages I am supposed to fill with chapter 1 due Monday. Today is Friday. Luckily, the entire rough draft isn't due until late January, and it's only November. "I have two whole months," I add out loud. Hipster guy looks up and raises an eye. Maybe he's listening to silence?

The phone vibrates again and again, bobbing in my bag between the chewing gum and the tampons. Do I want to know who it is? I twirl my pen. *Nope.*

Taking the cue from Hipster dude who hasn't stopped working save for his concern about me, I pop my ear buds in and blast the saddest love song I know, *Nothing Compares 2 U*, and begin to write chapter 1, title: The Break Up.

Mya's hands shake as she rushes to the front door and throws it open. Before she can speak, Dylan leaps up the two steps and barks, "What the hell were you thinking going to my mother and ratting on me? Now, I have to go to fucking rehab. I may be an asshole, but you're a nosy bitch!"

Maybe I should "reconsider" the word "fucking"? Hmmm...I chew on my pen for a moment but then go back at it:

Mya pushes him back down the stairs. "Shut up, Dylan. I don't need my parents to hear this, okay?" She grabs his arm and pulls him down the driveway.

I stifle a laugh because this is so not how it went down with me and Justin those few years ago when we broke up. He did come to my house to tell me he was being shipped off to military school (his mother was sick of him getting high all the time and blowing off school), but we actually wound up making out on my driveway right before he said goodbye...

But he yanks his arm away from her. "So, we have to protect your perfect parents, but my mom has to know everything?" A car roars by, quieting us for a moment.

When it's gone, Dylan runs his hands through his hair. "I told myself I wasn't going to do this," he says. "But you make me so mad sometimes. You always have to be right and I always have to be wrong. I always have to be the asshole." He turns around, jamming his hands in his pockets.

God, I loved it when he would do that. Shove his hands in his pockets. Adorable, with his silky black hair falling over his blue eyes. "Stop swooning, Hickman. Get it together," I whisper to myself.

Mya's heart swells and aches. "I'm sorry" she whispers to his back. "I'm sorry for telling your mother about everything. I just wanted to help you. I was scared."

He doesn't say anything.

I only wish I had been smart enough to say that to him. I was just scared and so I told his mom about the drugs.

She takes a step toward him and reaches out to touch him.

He turns around, his blue eyes cold and hard, and grabs her wrist. "I don't want your help. I don't need it. Just stay the fuck away from me."

Mya can't stop the tear as it rolls down her cheek. "Dylan—"

"We're over." He spits. "Don't call me. Don't follow me when I walk away."

The last few lines are more inspired by *Deprogramming Amy* who dumps her b-friend when he comes out to rescue her from the cult. "Don't follow me when I walk away," she tells him through her tears. Took my breath away, that scene did. Gripping.

I sit back and crack my knuckles again, a smile creeping on my face. Mrs. Dubois always tells me "show don't tell" and "show" is certainly what I just did.

·   ·   ·   ·   ·

Then the phone rings again, and I dig it out of my bag and finally pick it up. The number is from California.

"Bubbie?"

"Hi, Mad!"

"How's the sun?"

"Shining!"

"How's the beach?"

"Sandy!"

I close my eyes to imagine the beach in her backyard. "Mom got the tickets, Bub," I start to rap, "Going back to Cali…"

"Actually, that's why I called…"

My stomach sinks like when you expect an A on a paper, and you get it back and in big bold red ink it says *F*. "What's the matter?"

"I went to the doctor…and the long and short of it is I had a routine colonoscopy this week and they found a tumor." I hear a muffled sound like a sniffle or maybe a cough. She clears her throat. "They say it looks contained and that's a good thing. But, it's kind of large. The size of a fist."

I push the mouthpiece away and gulp. Bubbie takes a breath and says, "I'm having it taken out next week. Recovery will be a month." I hear the same muffled sound again. "You there, Maddie?"

"Yes," I squeak.

"Christmas vacation should still be fine, Maddie. As long as you don't expect me to walk across Golden Gate Bridge or anything." She attempts to laugh. As if.

Aside from that last line, there are these rare moments when Bubbie sounds so creepily like Mom. Moments of crisis where she talks like she's reading me a to-do list. Moments where I think, so they *are* related.

I look at the hand that's not holding the phone and it wants to grab something to hold on to. But there's nothing and no one there.

Except good old Hipster dude. He glances up from his laptop and smiles.

I try to smile a little like I'm on the phone with the boyfriend I don't have.

"Maddie?" My ear is enormous as I listen to my Bubbie tell me about her tumor stuck to her colon. She says something about possibly needing radiation but not being certain until the tumor is out and tested. Now my hands fly to my laptop.

I interrupt her, glad to actually have something to do, to say, to maybe offer her. Control. I know that's my M.O., but screw it. My grandmother is dying.

"Do you know if it's stage one, two or three because—" I scroll down and click on treatment. "The treatment varies depending on—"

"Sweetie, we don't know anything until after they take it out."

"The Mayo Clinic website says—"

"Madeline Jane Hickman…"

"—that even stage three and four have a decent prognosis with chemotherapy and they say that—"

"Maddie!" Her voice has the edge to it only reserved for when I obsess over something.

My call waiting beeps and cuts Bubbie off.

I pull the phone away and glance at the number. Barbara. Shit.

"Bubbie." I inhale and exhale like my shrink Josephine has instructed me to do. "I'm sorry. Okay. I'll chill out for a second."

"Good," I can hear her face relax. We have the same smile, wide, large teeth, full lips.

My eyes fill with tears: CANCER.

"Maddie, I'm not even really sick. This could just be a little nothing that they simply scoop out. I actually feel great."

I nod.

"We'll talk later. I love you, sweetie."

I breathe. "Love you, too."

I press the button and swallow all tears.

"Barbara?"

Big sigh.

Uh oh.

"Barb?"

"Yeah, hi. I just wanted to call you. Hey, did Bubbie call you? She left a message for me, and she sounded kind of weird." She lowers her voice, "Oh and Mom is up in her sewing room, trying to stitch the world straight for most of the day that I've been here doing my laundry. Anyway, I want to tell you something else."

"If you're going to tell me you've fallen off the wagon or that you even smelled alcohol, I will kill you. I swear I will. This is not the time."

"Ah, Maddie! Have a little faith. This is good news."

"I'm listening."

"I met someone! His name is Cliff and—wait, before you even try to tell me it's too soon after Michael and no I haven't told Mom..."

I pull the phone away and shut my eyes. What the hell is she talking about? God, there are so many times I just want to—

"...I like this guy. A lot."

"I gotta go, Barb. We can talk when I get home."

I press the end button on the phone and feel burning in the back of my throat, and I try to swallow the tears or indigestion or both. I put my phone into the pocket of my jeans and shove my notebook and pen into my leather backpack that Bubbie got me in London just this past summer. I look over at Hipster dude.

He pouts and shakes his head. "Gonna get one for the road?"

"Yeah. A latte." Then I add, "Extra sugar...extra foam."

·   ·   ·   ·   ·

No one is home when I get there. Good. I dash out to get Peter and Jack. Third wheel status is better than dealing with Things I Can't Do Anything About (Mom's compulsive sewing, Barb's love fantasies, Bubbie's cancer, especially Bubbie's cancer.)

CHAPTER THREE
PUT A CORK IN IT

Peter, Jack, and I spill out of the double doors and into the parking lot. The navy sky is dotted with stars. The air tastes fresh when I inhale.

Next to me, Peter bumps playfully into Jack. I dab my eyes with a rough movie theater napkin.

Jack says, "Poor Maddie", and Peter wraps a long arm over my shoulder. "You okay?"

"I'm fine." My nose honks when I blow into the napkin.

They continue ahead of me towards the car, leaning into each other, laughing. When Jack takes Peter's hand, my heart leaps. Wish I had someone to brush fingertips with. They stop walking and Peter pulls Jack towards him.

PDA overload. I shoot a hand into the air. "Hey, guys!" My hand falls.

Then out of the night emerges...A tall figure. I see the outline of a baseball hat and hear the jingle of car keys. The guy adjusts his hat, steps into the light coming from the movie theater, and I see a line of brown hair coming out from beneath the rim. He wears a flannel shirt.

Something about him kind of reminds me of...someone...Wait... is that?...Sean?

Sean.

Who I met two years ago, at my sister's wedding reception. I saw Sean on my way to the bathroom. He was sitting in a chair in the lobby, dressed in a white shirt and red tie like the rest of the waiters who had strolled around with trays of quiche and stuffed mushrooms during the cocktail hour. He was reading a book, *The Little Prince*, which turned out was research for a play he was doing at his high school. Within minutes we were trading favorite lines from the book and only stopped when my mother came out and growled at me to return to the party for the *Horah*.

Long story short, we tried to date but (what else is new) my delinquent ex-boyfriend haunted me. The end.

The frosty air makes me shiver. I try to walk so my clogs are noiseless on the asphalt. Jack opens the passenger side door of the car. I think of my promise to "go out with other boys", which I have yet to fulfill. Jack tosses the keys to Peter who chooses this moment to remember that I'm still here.

"Maddie, come on. It's freezing..."

I try to wave my hand at Peter to shut him up, but it's too late.

"Madeline?" Another voice says.

Madeline. Not Maddie. But *Madeline*.

"Sean?"

•   •   •   •   •

I've been in Sean's car for ten minutes but have managed to cover almost all of the last two years. "Slow down a minute." Sean puts a hand on the back of my seat. "I think I gotta recap: The end of your sophomore year, that Justin guy gets sent to military school, your sister goes off to rehab, and then you go to camp that summer and meet this new guy named—"

"Zak," I offer.

"Right, Zak who then *dies* in a car accident?"

"Yeah, on the way to meet me and my parents for dinner."

"My God, seriously?"

"Seriously."

Sean pulls his baseball hat off and puts it on his lap. His hair is tousled perfectly. "It probably makes for something to write about."

I laugh and play with the zipper of my jacket. Should I blast him with the rest?

What the hell? He hasn't run out of the car screaming yet.

"My shrink, Josephine—I see a shrink now, too, by the way. My shrink says that I'm in some kind of funk...still...and that I have to try to be more social...and not just with my best friends. Oh, and she thinks I'm using them as some kind of surrogate for a real relationship with a guy, which is kind of true because the idea of actually going on a real date with someone." I stop. But he's a captive audience so I start again, like a maniac. "It kind of, you know, scares me and then there's my sister who's getting divorced. I know, can you believe it? She practically just got married." I pause and let out the breath that I'd been holding in.

"Yeah," he smiles. "I was there."

I pause and take in the tiny freckle on Sean's jaw and how his mouth kind of frowns in a way that makes his lips puff out a bit. Sadly, these lovely details don't do anything but inspire me to keep talking, because, you know, I actually intend to scare off any heterosexual male who I have a remote possibility with.

"Michael always helped keep Barb sober and if she goes back to rehab, man, I don't know. That will be the third time. Yup, she was in and out and then back in last year." I take a breath, but all it does is fuel me to the finish line.

"Then there's my grandmother."

"Bubbie?"

"Yeah...Anyway, she just got news that she has these cysts in her colon, and she's having an operation like, next week and, of course, I researched all this online. Did you know that that colon cancer is the number one killer of people over the age of fifty-five, and she's well over that age."

Sean's face has the wide-eyed look of a deer who's about to kiss the front of a car. Maybe it's time for me to put a cork in it.

A few moments of awkward silence pass. Then I ask, "What's gone on with you?"

·   ·   ·   ·   ·

Sean brings me home and though he doesn't kiss me goodbye, little electrical impulses bounce between us when he hugs me. I snuggle right in before floating into the house.

In the mudroom, I slide out of my clogs and hang up my jacket. I walk through the hallway and living room to the stairs and go quietly up.

Through the cracked door of my mother's sewing room (a.k.a Barb's old room) a soft light beams from her favorite Victorian lamp.

Mom looks up from her needlepoint and smiles. Her hair is down and hangs in golden waves like my own hair.

"Hi, Mom."

"Hi, sweetie. I made a pot of chamomile. Thought you might want some before bed."

Gotta love my mom. "Thanks."

Mom sighs and lifts her hair from her forehead, which is dotted with sweat. "Ugh...hot flash..." She closes her eyes and covers her forehead and eyes. "Hon, can you get me—"

"Yeah. I'll be right back."

The routine is to get her a frozen washcloth. She has them in individual sandwich bags in the freezer. I run down the stairs and through the living room and foyer to the kitchen. Dad is there with the fridge door open.

"Hey, Dad. Thought you'd be in your study."

"There's only so much work I can do at this hour."

"Eating is better?"

He laughs. "Always. Especially—" He pulls out a plate that has some left-over sponge cake with strawberry toping. "*And* it's low fat!"

He puts the plate on the counter and opens the silverware drawer. He pulls out two forks. I take one, and we dig in silently.

"What about your deadline?" My father was asked to co-write a textbook on ocean waves and sound or something. He's been holed up in his study for months, every night.

He holds up a finger and finishes chewing. That's when I hear Mom yelling for me. Oh no! I stuff a large bite of cake and chew as I snatch open the freezer and grab a sandwich bag.

"She hot again?"

"Yeah," I dart out of the kitchen, leaving my father alone to his binge.

·   ·   ·   ·   ·

I take the stairs two at a time and hurry to the sewing room, dart through the doorway, and throw the baggy to Mom.

She catches the bag and rips it open. "Thanks, hon. God in heaven menopause just...sucks!"

This is torture for her; she used to only "glisten." Now she sweats.

I sit down on the rug in front of her. She drapes the washcloth over her forehead, closes her eyes, and leans back into her chair.

"Michael sent Barb the divorce papers today...already signed." She opens one eye and beams it at me. "He also sent a note saying he had safely arrived in Sudan and would be there until April. Oh, and after dinner, Barb sat Dad and I down and told us about this new Cliff fellow..."

I raise my eyebrows back.

Mom closes the eye and runs the washcloth all over her face, and I swear I see steam. "She didn't ask to move back in, thank God. Instead she told us that her friend from AA, Pam, is going to move into her apartment and help her with the rent. It seems that Barb may have a handle on this one. I swear she's using up the last of those nine lives of hers!"

I hug my knees.

"That leaves Bubbie." Mom puts the wet cloth on the side table next to her, careful that it rests on the plastic baggie and not the wood. "I spoke to her oncologist, and he thinks this will be very easy. An operation to remove the cyst and if it all looks clean and none of it has spread, they won't even do any chemo or radiation."

"Wow." I guess Barb isn't the only one with nine lives.

"It looks like while we have a few crises going, they are minor." But the crease on her forehead deepens.

Mom ticks off the "crises" like they are items on her to-do list she keeps posted on the side of the fridge. But I don't trust the universe. Something isn't right.

Yet I kind of want to pretend we can tic off those items, at least for now.

"How was your evening with Peter?"

I tell her all about Sean.

She is thrilled of course that I'm not mooning over the dead (Zak) or the delinquent (Justin). Another item she can tick off the list.

"It was fun." I look at my thumbnail and resist the urge to pull at the dry brittle cuticle; my mother will swat away my fingers before I even can contemplate picking at them.

I look back at Mom, and she smiles in a way that tells me she is ready to go to bed and only stayed up to see me. I rub my eyes and yawn. Stretch my legs out and my calf tightens. I point and flex my toes and remind myself to stretch tomorrow after my run.

She looks back down at her needlepoint and pulls at thread and then pushes the needle through. Without looking up she says casually, "Are you ready to send out any applications? Isn't Early Action soon?"

Before I can try to craft a reply, a piercing ache seizes my calf muscle.

I grab the muscle and see my mother's mouth move, but I don't hear her, like I pressed mute or something.

Then everything goes numb. Pulling my legs in and using my hands to hoist myself results in nothing. I'm floating or disconnected from my body.

What's happening?

The charley horse pain is compounded by this weird sensation that reminds me of when I sit in class for too long with my legs crossed and my feet fall asleep, only now it's in my hands and crawls up my arms to my jaw.

Anxiety attack.

I get them every once in a while, but this is completely different. Oh my God. I'm dying! My chest is so heavy, and I try to grab at my heart and make sure it is still beating, but moving my hands, moving anything, is impossible.

"Sweetie?" Mom reaches over and brushes the hair out of my eyes. I didn't know I had hair in my eyes. I push my leg straight to break the cramp. It snaps back and I'm afraid I've broken it! I'm a writhing ball with twitching arms and legs. I hear Mom say make sure she's breathing. Epileptic fit. Call the doctor. Someone, call the doctor! I roll across the room, a scream echoing in my head. What if I bite my tongue? Tumble down the stairs? One false move and it's over. But nothing else happens except that the numbness in my jaw tightens the hinges like someone squirted crazy glue in my mouth. I think of that *Medical Incredible* show where a guy had a seizure and before he had it, he felt numbness and tingling in his face.

Oh God! I'm having a seizure?

It's like I'm free falling from a cliff only nothing is happening. Nothing is happening, everything is happening... I'm losing it... dying... going insane... rolling out the door and into the hallway. What the hell... am I doing... oh my god oh my god oh my god—

"Stan! Stan!" Mom sounds panicked. "Stanley, Stanley! Get up here! Get up here now!"

I can't make out if Dad responds, but Mom kneels down so her face is near mine. I guess I've stopped rolling. She turns so her ear is pressed against my mouth. I smell lilac. "Can you breathe, honey?"

I nod, unable to unhinge the trap door of my mouth. I hear the sound of heavy feet running quickly up the stairs. The door opening.

"Bernice? What's going on?" I imagine that Dad looks down and sees what might appear to be a corpse, and his wife trying to revive the dead body of his daughter. Shit, I could die! Never before, even when Zak died, did I really *get* that *I* could die. Now I do.

My parents talk to each other in loud, panicked tones. High-pitched voices punctuated by "Maddie!" (Mom) "Maddie, can you hear me?" (Dad). I want to say, "Yes, yes I hear you," but I'm trapped inside my head.

"She just...and then...I don't know!"

"It's probably just...I know, I know it's scary...she's breathing and even her color is fine... Let's do that."

That's all I hear, and the words don't connect to any meaning. Some kind of alien invaded my body and the Maddie who I thought I was is gone. Gone.

I want her back.

•   •   •   •   •

I hear a grunt and smell strawberry and vanilla and coffee. My father's face is close enough to see the light, reddish blond stubble tinged with gray. I'm surprised he can hold me. We move slowly. Mom's behind us shuffling in her slippers.

We travel down the hallway. My father nudges my bedroom door open with his foot. It's dark and cool, the lavender and white checked headboard of my bed appears dark and one color. He lays me down, on the bedspread, a comfortable, familiar softness. My mother and I picked everything out together last year. I had said to her, "Why are we bothering to redo my room? I'll be gone soon." She laughed and said, "You don't redo a room with the intention of permanence, Mad." I had no idea what she meant, but for some reason it makes sense to me now. That was one of the best days I had had with Mom. Her decorating was something I resisted for years, and there we were doing it together.

The disconnection and the fear of dying are gone, for now. My parents whisper to each other as they stand at the foot of my bed. My head is heavy. I can't hold it up.

So, I don't.

CHAPTER FOUR
TILL IT STOPS BEATING

My eyes open. I stare into the darkness for a little while. I turn my head to see the clock but something, maybe a tissue, is blocking it. My right calf muscle twinges. I reach down to touch it but instead touch sweatpants. I don't remember putting them on. I close my eyes and fall asleep.

. . . . .

The room is lighter now. I turn to my side and am seized by a coldness that wraps around my body. I curl into a "c" and put the heel of my hand in my mouth to stop the scream that rises in my throat. Weirdness creeps over me. It's like I'm disappearing, shrinking, getting smaller and younger. I'm six years old and have woken up in the middle of the night from a nightmare where I can't find my mother in a department store. I want to run up to my parents' room, but I'm too afraid to get out of bed.

. . . . .

Sunbeams stream through the window warming my body. I'm on my side, with my hand tucked under my cheek. My cheek hurts. I lift my head and rub it. I hear the water running and dishes clanking, muffled voices talking from down the hall.

My stomach growls. I think of Friday. Sitting with Sean in his car. Peace with the edges of excitement fills me. I flip open the covers to get out of bed. And then—

Everything else about Friday, in my mother's sewing room and then my dad carrying me downstairs...

It falls on me like a garbage truck dumping all the garbage from a street into a landfill, and I'm the landfill. I see the clock and can only make out the first number. *Nine.*

Oh God.

Then the rest spills out of the back of my brain.

It's Wednesday.

I slept my way through Saturday, Sunday, Monday, and yesterday. My mother woke me briefly to eat from a tray. Chicken soup and toast. I would look at the clock intermittently, and it was usually 1 pm or 8 pm. I did watch a little TV, only when I ate, and I can remember seeing an episode of some make-over reality show. This very heavy blonde woman who was a Paris Hilton impersonator and she wanted to separate from that identity...It was weird because I had seen an episode of another reality show with the same woman, but in that one she wanted to become a celebrity impersonator. Kind of made me think reality shows are totally fake. But, I watched the make-over show anyway.

Peter, Susan, and Barb all called, and with each one she would stand there and talk into the phone: "No, no, she's still not feeling well. Yes, I will. I'll have her call you when she's better." And then later, when they all called for the four millionth time: "It must be the flu." With Barb, Mom finally said, "Yeah...something has hit her hard...We're not sure, but we think it was a panic attack, like the ones Dad used to get."

I'm still staring at the 9. It's blurry now from the water in my eyes. Smells of eggs, bacon, and toast. Are they making it for me? I know that while my family used to be great at ignoring major problems, we have all had enough therapy to know that what happened Friday and what's happening right now with me, cannot be denied.

I remember yesterday after my mother came in at some point during the end of the day, I only know it was the end because the natural light in the room was pretty dim. She came in with my father. He whispered, "Is she awake?"

"No, she's still sleeping," my mom whispered back. Then I heard the rattle of the spoon against the bowl as she picked up my tray. "She's been eating, and I know she's getting up to go the bathroom."

"This is exactly what happened to me." Dad's voice was barely a whisper. "Only I was alone. My Aunt Sarah came by, but Dad was with Mom at the hospital. I stayed like this, sleeping and for an entire week. Then Dad came back and made me go to school."

I had the covers over my face and was on my side. I peered through the slit of the blanket and saw them at the doorway.

"I say we give her one more day and then I'm bringing her to that doctor Josephine recommended." Mom didn't whisper this time.

I almost yelled, what doctor and when did you talk to Josephine?

But I didn't. I fell asleep.

·　　·　　·　　·　　·

The numbers on the clock are clear. The panic is gone, but my head throbs. I want a Tylenol or a hammer to bang out the pain. A small part of me says, get out of bed. This all would make a great journal entry. At least write something.

But I'm frozen. What if this happens at school? What if this happens when I see Sean again? What if this happens when I'm driving?

I can't be alone or leave the house. Forget it.

I hear footsteps coming down the hallway, and they stop in front of my room. I see the shadow of them under the doorway.

A knock.

"Mad?"

Dad.

"Sweetie?"

Mom.

I take a deep breath. The fear drains out a little, but the head-pounding is louder.

"I'm awake. I have a bad headache."

They open the door and walk towards my bed with eyebrows knitted.

"Oh, honey bunch," Dad reaches down and touches my head lightly.

"I'll get you some Tylenol." Mom hustles back out, probably grateful to do something instead of looking at me. I know she wants to haul me out of bed and drop me off at the nearest shrink.

Dad sits on the edge of the bed. "How are you feeling otherwise?"

I don't know how to answer. The humming sound from my clock takes up the empty space of the silence.

Then Dad says, "Look, Mad, I think we should take you to the doctor. Maybe get a checkup and also maybe see a...a psychiatrist."

"What about Josephine?"

"She's just a therapist. You know you might need something. Maybe medication."

"What?" Everyone I know on medication, kids at school, those people are really screwed up. They have ADD or some kind of depression thing. Am I that messed up? Didn't this *just* happen to me? I've never had a breakdown or been messed up. This is what I get? Barb goes ignored for years, and they let her do whatever she wanted. Me, I mess up once and they throw me to a Super Shrink.

My father touches my arm and says, "Honey, listen. We just want you to be okay. Believe me, I wish I had some of those medications available when I was younger."

I want to ask him about his mother in the hospital, but Mom comes back with two Tylenol and water. I take them and drink the water. No one says anything.

·   ·   ·   ·   ·

"You won't come in to see me?" We've only been on the phone a few seconds, yet even the soothing sound of Josephine's voice sends me into panic.

I breathe in and out. I hold the phone with a shaky hand.

"You won't leave the house?" I shake my head, unable to talk.

"I know you're there, and you're crying."

I sniffle.

"Your mom filled me in. You're just scared of having the panic attacks again."

I nod and sniffle.

"You know all those breathing exercises I gave will work with even the worst panic attack."

I try to talk, but the tears are flooding into my mouth now.

"Writing would be a good thing right now too..."

I stay very still.

"Look, we both know that anxiety has been a good friend to you at times. It's your alarm system that you have to slow down and detach, get some space."

I make an *mmhmmm* noise because I want to just get off the phone. And can't even begin to think about what I need to "slow down" about or get "some space" over.

Josephine sighs. "Can you put your mother back on?"

I hand the phone to my mother. Her blue eyes are red with dark bags under them.

·   ·   ·   ·   ·

"Have you even showered?" Barb's voice is filled with disbelief.

I hold the phone to my ear. "I just did."

"Good." She sounds relieved. As if showering were the ultimate indication of my mental health. "What about school? I can't believe you would blow off school."

I close my eyes and smell the rose water soap I borrowed from Mom. "I don't know." Here come those tears again. "I...can't leave the house, Barb."

She sighs, not irritated more kind of sad. "This is bad. This is really bad. What about Josephine or something?"

I open my eyes and the tears spill. "I spoke to her. She talked, and I cried...I couldn't leave the house to even have Mom take me to my appointment on Monday."

"What did she say?" I picture Barb's tiny hands waving or pointing as she talks and her toffee eyes wide.

"Not much. But she did say I need to see a psychiatrist and that I need to get to see her." I pull at a thread from my bathrobe. "She offered to come to the house."

"So, let her!" Another sigh and I picture her rubbing her forehead. "And go to the doctor too."

"I don't know. I just feel so awful unless I'm sleeping."

"What happened?"

"I don't know."

"I'm supposed to be the fucked up one, not you." She laughs. I don't.

"How are things with Cliff," I ask hoping the answer is brief.

"Good. We are taking it slow for now." Nothing else.

Who's the fucked up one now?

.   .   .   .   .

"I have your books. Can I come over? Susan's dying to see you. She has this scholarship essay she has to write and wants your help." Peter has his high pitch nervous voice on. Through the phone line, I picture his face—scared, wide-eyed.

I don't reply. There's no way the senior class most-likely-to-be the first female president needs my help.

"She doesn't actually need your help," he confesses. I know he's sweating. I know he's pacing too. I know that Jack may even be with him and that they are probably at Peter's house "studying" because his parents aren't home.

I pull covers over me and shut my eyes. "Don't worry about me. I'll be fine. Say hi to Jack." Click.

.   .   .   .   .

"Peter filled me in. You're going all loopy-nut job on us? You know what? It's about time. I mean you friggin' intellectualize yourself into feeling fine."

I lie on my side. I wouldn't have picked up the phone if I had checked the caller ID and seen that it was Susan. I only picked up the phone because I thought it was Mom calling to say she was on her way home from her client's house. It's weird to be alone...what if I have another attack? The thought sends numbness down my back, and so I clutch at the covers, at the soft satin and fleece blanket Mom wrapped me in before she left.

"Maddie?"

"Oh, uh, what?"

"Peter told me about Sean..."

I twist the covers and pull them up to my nose not wanting to think about that night...since I probably won't ever leave the house, leave this room, leave this bed...

"Hello?"

"Sorry...Yeah, we had a nice time hanging out."

"So?"

"So, I don't know. I'm kind of busy being loopy nut job, right?"

We both laugh, and I'm normal for a second.

"He seems to like you no matter what kind of drama is going on in your life. He's a keeper."

"He is."

We don't say anything else for a minute, the phone line buzzes faintly, and before I hang up, I tell her, "Give me a few days and maybe we can go over your essay."

. . . . .

As I doze off again, and this time I do think about Sean and I think about that he hasn't called. It's been a week. But I guess it doesn't matter. What could I say to him? I'm not the same person I was a week ago.

This time I dream. I dream about Zak and Justin. They are having coffee, at my favorite coffee shop in town. I'm standing in the doorway so excited to see them both. But when I approach their table, they don't look at me. I say hello but nothing. I reach out to touch them and they fade. I scream.

"Madeline?"

Someone grabs my ankle and squeeze. The hands are rough and large. I once saw Dad do that to Barb one Saturday morning, years ago when Barb was always nursing a hangover on a Saturday morning. A hang over that my parents would call, "worked too late." Only Barb didn't work late every Friday night at the mall.

"Madeline?" He says again.

I open my eyes and turn my head to look at him.

"Hi, Dad."

"Hi," his voice is scratchy. "I heard you scream. You're okay?" He strokes my head.

The dream came back to me in a fast-forward rush. Justin's blue eyes and Zak's *jewfro*, as he used to call it. I swallow and nod my head.

"Want to go get a late lunch? We could make a run to that great diner in Stamford." He looks hopeful, but I shake my head. I can't. I just can't do it.

"How about we sit together in the kitchen, and I make some grilled cheese sandwiches with lots of butter?" I smile. I haven't eaten anything like that for a few years. He forgets I'm almost eighteen. But since I'm clearly not acting eighteen, I let him help me out of bed and go into the kitchen.

It's the first time I've left my room for longer than a few minutes since Friday. I think it gives us both hope. We eat in silence. Actually, he eats and I pick. We share the paper, which has only bad news that as soon as I read, I'm a pile of crap all over again. As I go back to my room, Dad sighs.

So do I.

· · · · ·

When Mom comes home she tells me Mrs. Dubois called and the guidance secretary called.

"What did you tell them?"

"That you're sick."

"Oh." She stares at me again with red lines in her eyes. "I'm tired," I tell her.

"No, you're not, Maddie, and Monday this is all going to end. We're going to the doctor."

· · · · ·

Later, I'm in the hallway on my way to get a glass of water. They're about to cook dinner. I hear pots and pans clanging:

"I'm not going to let another daughter slide away, Stan."

"Sweetie, Maddie is not Barbara. She's not drinking or doing anything self-destructive."

"Yeah, not yet, but if we don't nip this whole thing now, God knows what will happen."

Silence.

"You know, Bern, your mother was right."

Another silence. I walk forward to hear better.

"Helen's right about this. We might have to let Maddie fall apart."

Silence and pans tapping the stove. Mom's voice is softer. "Do you think it was Mom's cancer? Do you think that's what tipped it all for Maddie?"

My father's voice is just as soft, so I step forward a bit more. "I don't know." I hear a kiss sound. I picture him putting his arm around Mom's shoulders and kissing her head, like I have seen him do a lot of times. "It could have been that moment you were asking about college. It could have been her night out with her friends. It could have been anything."

I walk to the bathroom and sit down on the closed toilet, my head in my hands.

·　·　·　·　·

I can't believe it, but since my attack last Friday, I've totally pushed Bubbie's cancer out of my mind. I don't know how a person can forget about cancer. I don't know how me, Maddie Hickman, neurotic obsessive about my family, about anyone I love, and Maddie, totally petrified of dying, how I, the very same Maddie, could forget.

I'm awake and craving a latte when the phone rings. I pull the covers off my head and tuck them under my arms. I look over at the phone and see Bubbie's name flash up: H. Kurland. My eyelid ticks. It's been doing that all morning, whenever I am awake. Great. Not only do I have some kind of attack thing going on, but now I have Tourette's.

Tourette's makes me think of Zak, who had these funny jaw ticks. The phone is still ringing. Zak. Bubbie. Zak is dead. Bubbie is—

I snatch the phone from my bed stand.

"Hi, Bub," I press speaker so I can snuggle back under the covers.

"Hi, sweetie." Pause. "Mom told me you had an attack of some kind?"

"Yeah, I think I'm going to the nut house next."

"Want to tell me what's wrong?"

I stare at my curtains, the floral print, purple and pink petals and leaves of green blurs. I close my eyes. Should have just done the simple dotted Swiss. *Stuck. The words. Stuck in my throat.*

"I-have-to-go," I finally croak out, confused.

"Honey? Sweetie, talk to me."

I want to hang up the phone.

"Listen, your father, I remember, used to get these terrible panic attacks. There was a time before you were born. He had this period of just not wanting to leave the house. He even took some time off."

I struggle, the panic overwhelming me. I push myself to an upright position. I don't want to hear this right now. Maybe going crazy is in the family.

"Honey? Are you still there? Listen, just breathe."

I do as she says and force myself to breathe in and out of my mouth. My eye continues to tic. After a few moments, I hear her breathing with me.

"Can you talk?"

"Yeah." The tic continues but my chest isn't as tight.

"Good, that's good."

"Wow, Bubbie, that was weird."

"I know, I know. Listen, honey, just keep trying to breathe, and I can call you later."

Cancer. I remember again. "Wait! When's the operation?"

"On Monday. And don't worry. I've got all my friends here to help me through and really, I feel good! I'll have Joyce call you guys with updates throughout the day."

"I just wish we could be there with you."

"Honey, I'd rather see you when I'm recovered and can take you to poetry readings at Custom House Coffee or go grab a bite together at that new Vietnamese restaurant. And, of course, we have to finally make our walk across the Golden Gate Bridge."

"Okay," I nod. Tears flow. I wipe my nose. "I just...you have to do everything you can to make sure that you don't...because I don't know what I will do if you...you." I can't say it.

"Oh, sweetie." Now I hear her sniffle. "Never worry about your heart honey, till it stops beating."

"Bubbie! That's horrible! Did you come up with that?"

"No. E.B. White. And it's not horrible. All it means is that I am alive right now. Alive and not really sick, even. And the truth is, if we are alive and feeling things, life is going to hurt sometimes. But for now, honey, my heart is beating just fine."

We both cry and then at the same time laugh.

"I love you honey!"

"I love you, Bub!"

After we hang up, I tuck myself into my bed and fall asleep.

CHAPTER FIVE
"HOW CRAZY WAS YOUR MOTHER?"

"Hey."

The weight of my eyelids makes me open them slowly. Standing in my doorway is a shadow in the semi-darkness.

"Dad," my throat is dry.

He walks into my room carefully stepping over the decorative pillows scattered on the floor. He opens the drapes and then pulls the soft blinds so light slices through.

I didn't sleep the entire day. Good.

"What time is it?" I ask.

"A little past two." He opens the other set of shades. "How about some lunch? Mom made lentil soup."

I try to remember the last time I ate. I woke up this morning at six and had coffee with my mother before she went for her power walk. But then I fell back asleep.

"Yeah, soup sounds good."

I sit up, brush the sleep from my eyes and face. I'm ready to ask: "Dad, how crazy was your mother?"

He laughs. "Oh, boy. Let's discuss this over soup. This is not a conversation for an empty stomach."

I laugh.

"Okay."

Minutes later I sit at the table and share a loaf of bread with my father. I have a small cup of steaming lentil soup under my nose.

"Mom is at work this afternoon." Dad hands me a large soupspoon and then sits across from me.

"You get to babysit?"

He chuckles.

We spoon soup, the metal clinking against the bowls like the driftwood wind chimes on our porch. When I glance up at Dad, I see he has a chunk of bread stuck to his chin. I resist reaching over and wiping his mouth like my mother sometimes does.

"Let's see. Where do I begin?" He reaches for more bread. With Dad, there's no bread knife there's just the "rip and dip" method as he calls it when he eats Mom's famous soup and bread.

"Just tell me what the deal was with the crazy part. Did she talk to voices in her head? Did she have these attacks like you and me have?" I tuck my hair behind me ears.

Dad scratches his head. Then his face changes to what I call his professor face but then it flashes to another face. All his features fall.

"I loved my mother. She was a total lunatic, but I loved her." He chuckles. "She was so crazy. You know we were poor, I mean the kind of poor where my mother owned the same house dresses for at least the eighteen years I was home. So poor we used to reuse tea bags for an entire week. So poor that when I had my bar mitzvah, we used the money I got from relatives and friends to pay for the party that we had in the basement of the temple."

He sits back and folds his arms over his small, pot belly.

"And I admit they were backwards. We didn't call Mother crazy though. At least not until later, after she died." He looked at me like I forgot this entire story, but this part I knew:

"She played piano by ear and had these great jobs playing at local pubs. But she screwed it up every time. She wouldn't wear a real dress, just those housecoats. Even though she played incredibly, she was fired after a few nights. She stopped completely before I finished elementary school."

I put my spoon down.

"Father brought her home one night, and he had her wrapped up in one of his long trench coats. She was crying, and he was cursing her under his breath. I was sleeping upstairs, but those row houses, the walls were paper thin." He runs his hand over his face, the crumbs fall away from his lips. He looks old to me with the light from the glass chandelier bouncing off his eyes.

"She had gone to the club in one of those house coats and one of the managers gave her a dress to put on. She completely lost it and ripped off all her clothes and ran out on stage to play. Father was working at the plant that night, but they called him to come get her. He was fired for leaving and Mother never played again."

He stares at his empty bowl and his eyes are red.

"Dad," I say softly. "What happened to her then?"

"They put her away, and she died a few years later."

"Did you get to visit her?"

"Yeah..." I can see that whatever happened in those visits, he doesn't want to talk about.

His face changes again, and he looks like a professor. "She was mentally ill but back then they didn't call it anything. They gave her all the wrong medicines. If she were alive today, she would have therapy and the right medication."

I don't know what to say. My problems seem small. Can't get over ex-boyfriend. Can't think about college. Obsession with googling That Which I Have No Control Over. Constantly worried about everyone around me. But I do wonder if I have what she had and if it's only because I live in the twenty-first century that I'm not locked up.

Dad and I silently do the dishes and he disappears up to his study but before he goes he says, "Maddie, you aren't my mother. You don't have her life."

"But I read that anxiety can be hereditary."

"And so is alcoholism."

I don't say anything.

"And you aren't an alcoholic."

I considered that. "But that's 'cause I don't drink."

"Right. But you don't drink because you are aware of what it could do to you."

"How am I supposed to avoid anxiety?"

"I don't think you avoid it, but you can prevent it from getting out of control."

"What do you mean?"

He walks over and strokes my hair. "You need to see the doctor and most importantly, go back to school."

.   .   .   .   .

Later, sitting on my bed, I stare out the window at the streetlights glowing in the dark starless sky. A shiver of fear runs down my arms, and I hug myself thinking about the things I love to do like run, or write at a coffee shop, and how now those seem impossible.

CHAPTER SIX
THE DOCTOR IS IN

My eyes travel over the pale blue walls lined with wainscoting of Dr. Foster's office and then land on the small clock on the wall. Monday the 18th. 8 am, 11 am Pacific Time. While Bubbie is being wheeled into the operating room, I'm about to learn my psychological state.

Mom still smells faintly of hot iron. She dressed up a little for the doctor or maybe it's for a client she hasn't told me about this afternoon. Dad sits at the edge of the white chair with his arms crossed.

I look at the scatter of magazines on the table before us. *Highlights*, *US*, *People*, and *The New Yorker*: The young, the stupid, and the intellectual. That just about covers everyone who will probably show up to this office.

In the corner of the waiting room is a small white noise machine. A basket of hard candy sits on the table next to us. My mouth tastes rancid, so I lean over, barely standing to reach for a mint. Mom re-crosses her legs. Dad's eyes are closed. I think of Bubbie again and what she said to me last night, "Tomorrow is a big day for us both. We have to let other people do their jobs and help us. We have to. No choice." Amen.

"Madeline Hickman?"

I haven't even unwrapped the mint yet. I stuff it in my dirty sweatshirt pocket. I'm the only person besides my parents in the waiting room, so I find it funny the receptionist says my name.

I stand up, self-conscious of my appearance. The baggy, saggy look as my mother lovingly referred to it under her breath right before we left the house. This is certainly not becoming of a "together" person. But then again,

I guess I'm not that together, and maybe I should just kind of embrace it. I don't know. I hope my deodorant works because I haven't showered. I lift my purse and put it over my shoulder. I don't even know why I brought it. Habit. I haven't driven since last week or even checked my cell phone or email either.

As I walk past Mom and Dad, they throw me looks that say, want us to come with you? I shake my head. The receptionist leads me past her desk and through two more closed doors, around a short hallway, and to an open door. I peer into the room and see a large leather chair and a framed picture on the wall. It's a cartoon drawing of the most awesome penguin character in the world. *Opus*. He is sort of floating with the word "why" in thought bubbles around him. Thanks to my dad, who has some collectors' books of the comic strip *Outland*, I'm practically certified in all things *Opus*. I laugh.

"What's so funny?" And there he is. I've never met with a psychiatrist before, and I thought he'd be wearing a suit or a doctor's white coat. But instead a short man with a gray ponytail, wearing a small diamond earring emerges from another door in the room.

Before I open my mouth, a flood of forgotten things come to me: I have an essay due in AP English on Monday, I haven't heard from Sean, and I was supposed to have the final edited copy of the literary magazine in Mrs. Dubois's hands yesterday.

"What's so funny?" Dr. Foster asks again. His face and voice match each other well. Mild is the word that comes to me.

"Oh, uh...I love *Opus*." My purse dangles from my hand.

"Isn't that before your time?"

"My dad has a bunch of books."

He smiles so that his eyes practically disappear. I step all the way into the room and see the leather chair is diagonal from a couch and across from a large desk.

"Take a seat." He gestures to the couch.

I sit on the end closest to the door. He sits in the chair.

"So," he folds his hands together.

I cross my legs like my mother does because I don't know what to say or what he wants me to say.

His smile stays, his face so pleasant, with the crinkly smallish eyes and ponytail. We sit like this for another few moments. Then he says, "You want to tell me what brings you into my office today?"

No. But I nod my head.

He cocks his head to the side, waiting.

I can't seem to find any words to begin so I shake the leg that's crossed.

He continues to smile, but his eyes narrow onto the shaking leg.

I stop and uncross, re-cross my legs the other way.

He leans forward and says, "Just begin with how you feel right now."

I think for a minute but inside it's all white paper, blank, nothing. "I don't know."

"Your mother told me that you had a panic attack recently?"

I nod.

"Why don't you tell me about that?"

We look at each other and I hear the sound of something ticking faintly and then even more faint is the white noise machine in the waiting room.

He gives me another gentle smile and for some reason that's when I find my voice. I tell him everything that's happened since last Friday. When I'm done, I slump back into the couch.

"Nothing like that has ever happened before?" He asks.

"Nothing that lasted long. I mean I've had little panic attacks but nothing that really scared me." I smooth the messy bun I threw my hair into this morning.

He nods and reaches back to his desk and pulls out a sheet from a drawer and grabs a clipboard from the desk. "I'm going to ask you a bunch of questions. There's no wrong answer."

I nod.

"Now, tell me if the statement I read is always true, never, or sometimes."

I have done this with Josephine before, so I know what I'm about to get into. I look at Opus behind Dr. Foster. I wish I could make out all of the words not just "why."

"'I do things slowly.', " Dr. Foster begins.

"Umm…" I haven't done anything but eat, sleep, and pee lately. But none of that has been particularly slow so I answer:

"Sometimes."

"'My future seems hopeless.'"

Lately... "Yes, I mean always."

He nods without looking up. Ugh, it's hot in here. Oh God I hope I don't get an attack here. I start to unzip my sweatshirt.

"'The pleasure and joy has gone out of my life.'"

"Yes. I mean always." I wiggle out of the sweatshirt and put it on my lap.

"'I have difficulty making decisions.'"

"No."

"'I have lost interest in aspects of life that used to be important to me.'"

I haven't run since last Friday morning. "Yes." I stare at the comic strip and squint to try again and make out the other words but all I see is "why", "why."

"'I feel sad, blue, and unhappy.'" *Why, why, why...*

...And frustrated and scared. "Yes. Sometimes."

"'I am agitated and keep moving around.'" *Why.*

"No, never." I tear my eyes away and look right into Dr. Foster's. They are blue, blue like Justin's. Blue like my mom's.

"'I feel fatigued.'"

Focus! "Always."

"'It takes great effort for me to do simple things.'"

No, no just the hard things like leaving the house. "Sometimes."

"'I feel that I am a guilty person who deserves to be punished.'"

I laugh.

He finally looks up with that same slightly amused look. "I take that as a never?"

"Never."

"'I feel like a failure.'"

I want to tell him I'm too scared to feel failure or guilt. "Sometimes." I answer.

"I have one more questionnaire, and then we can talk some more."

I nod. Even though I'm hot, my heart is steady. I grip the sweatshirt in my lap. The panic monster has been locked in a closet. I know he's there, but safely away. For now.

Dr. Foster rapid fires the next set of questions. Most of which get a *yes*:

"'Do you experience sudden episodes of intense and overwhelming fear that seem to come on for no apparent reason?'"

"'During these episodes, do you experience symptoms similar to the following: racing heart, chest pain, difficulty breathing, choking sensation, lightheadedness, tingling or numbness?'"

"'During the episodes do you worry about something terrible happening to you, such as embarrassing yourself, having a heart attack or dying?'"

"'Do you worry about having additional episodes?'"

I begin to sweat. He continues:

Have you experienced or witnessed a frightening, traumatic event, either recently or in the past?

Do you continue to have distressing recollections or dreams of the event?

Do you become anxious when you face anything that reminds you of that traumatic event?

Do you try to avoid those reminders?

Do you have any of the following symptoms: difficulty falling or staying asleep, irritability or outbursts of anger, difficulty concentrating, feeling "on guard", easily startled?

I laugh and almost answer "yes" to this one because of my googling habit:

Do you engage in any repetitive behaviors (like hand washing, ordering, or checking) or mental acts (like praying, counting, or repeating words silently) in order to end intrusive thoughts or images?

Dr. Foster fills in the answer to the last question and then looks at it briefly before putting it on his desk. I relax my shoulders a bit and sink further into the couch.

"Can you tell me what you think about these attacks?" He leans back in his chair, which squeaks a little.

I think I'm crazy. But I can't say that. Instead I say, "I think my parents want me to take some medicine. I just want these attacks to stop."

"Before we go to the medication discussion, I think we should talk a bit about the attacks and then have you get a complete physical, just to rule out anything."

The panic swoops down on me and I clench up, wrapping my sweatshirt around myself. "What do you mean? Like what? Like a seizure or something?"

"Oh, no. Probably not. I have all patients get physicals before the medication conversation, anyway. Standard procedure."

"I need medicine?"

He smiles patiently. "You might. But I think this is up to you. You're almost an adult."

"Not till June."

"That's not that far away."

The terribleness washes all over me again. My throat tightens. "Yeah," I croak. "Tell me about it."

"What are your plans for college?"

"Uh...I applied to a bunch of places." I'm lying, but the confession lodged in my throat is about to erupt. "I wrote the applications. Some. I need to send them out."

"Oh? How come you haven't sent them?"

He looks me directly in the eye and I squirm. "Well...uh...I..."

"Um..." Then before I know it, I tear up and then full on cry. I don't want my parents to hear. I think of the white noise machine gratefully.

Dr. Foster pushes the tissue box towards me.

I smile weakly at him and wipe my nose.

"I have a diagnosis. Are you ready?"

I nod, weak from crying.

"Separation anxiety." His voice is calm and even.

"Separation anxiety?" I curl my fingers around the tissue. "Does that mean I might start sucking my thumb again?"

"Only if you want to."

"Hmmmm..."

"It means you are afraid to leave the nest." Dr. Foster says but his face is calm, almost amused.

"The nest?"

"The nest," he confirms.

I look at Opus and his thoughts bubbles. *Afraid to leave the nest. Why?*

Chapter Seven
In the Clear

That afternoon, I wake up from a long nap to Mom standing at the foot of my bed, tears in her eyes, but smiling. She hands me the phone. "It's Bubbie. Good news!"

I take the phone. "Hello?"

"Sweetie! Guess what?" Her voice is groggy but excited. "We're in the clear! They scooped out my enormous tumor, which was contained! Home-free and no radiation or anything required! Just recovery from the operation! I'm looking forward to my friends waiting on me hand and foot!"

By now I'm sitting up, the sleep gone from my eyes. Mom is grinning. She leans over and says into the phone, "We can make those plans for Christmas now!"

"Absolutely!"

The rest of the afternoon and evening I do normal things. Read some of my history textbook and even work on an essay for English. I watch that same reality make-over show, which normally makes me laugh. But today the host screamed at this girl for wearing acid wash jean shorts and fishnet stockings together, instead of following the "guidelines of style" presented earlier in the episode. My heart started to pound again. Poor girl wasn't ready to venture out of her comfort zone. I can relate. I had to flip to a home make-over show on HGTV. Simmered that anxiety way down to a dull boil.

Before I go to sleep that night, Mom sits at the edge of my bed. "Come with me to work tomorrow. It's a safe way to begin venturing out."

"Sure." Even though a little tremor of uncertainty writhes in my stomach, I know it's time to start living again. "Sure. That sounds good."

·　　·　　·　　·　　·

Perfumed and powdered, smelling of Chanel, Mom stands in front of the large window of her office that faces downtown. On her enormous desk, is a sample of a squash-colored "flora dora" design fabric, a large leather notebook, and her laptop. My eyes are heavy, and my body slumped into the upholstered couch, in shock from all the movement it has bared on this early morning trip into the City. I lift a heavy arm to reach for a mug of that tea rests on a wooden coaster.

The buzzer rings. Client *numero uno* has arrived. Mom walks to the intercom next to the door of the office. She presses it and says, "Come on up, Eleanor."

Moments later I hear the sharp tap of heels clacking down the hallway of the building. When "Eleanor" comes rushing into the office, she is at least six feet tall and reeks of some unfamiliar floral scent.

"Bernice!"

They cheek kiss but it looks like Mom is a child reaching up to kiss an adult.

"How are you, Eleanor?" Mom oozes charm and ease. But I'm certain any client who insists on meeting at 7:30 on a Friday morning is anything but easy. "This is my daughter, Madeline." I stand up and smile.

"Oh, how wonderful!" Eleanor scans my body and her eyes rest on my face. "Ooh! You've got great bone structure! Tall, too, and thin. Ever think of modeling?"

If I had the coffee, I would spit it out. Mom shoots me a "be polite" look. I force a reply, "Thanks. No, I haven't thought of modeling."

Eleanor shrugs off her mink coat and strikes a pose, her long limbs and flat stomach making her look thirty years younger. She smiles revealing too-white fake teeth and there's not one wrinkle line around her mouth.

"Twenty-five years on the runway. Paid for college for all my kids and my ex-husbands!" She gives a husky laugh and turns back to my mother.

"Mom, I can go get scones and coffee for you two." I reach up and smooth any fly away hairs from my ponytail.

"Sure, sweetie, that would be great."

"Oh, just coffee for me! Gotta keep my model figure!"

She flashes her veneers at me.

"Excuse me," I say and flash back a polite smile before rushing out of the office. Panic kind of lives on the edge of me as I walk as fast as I can to the elevator. While I wait for it to come, I put my hand in my pocket and feel for the bottle of Rescue Remedy that I've been carrying around since Monday afternoon. Dr. Foster was the one who suggested I also take this stuff. We went and got it right after the appointment. It's supposed to provide you a kind of calming when you take it under the tongue, and you can take it as often as you need it.

Once the door opens to the elevator and I step in and see it's empty, I take the dropper out and put fifteen drops under my tongue. *Rescue me, please!* The doors open and I step out into the lobby.

I walk quickly out of the building and down a block, barely breathing in the perfume that whooshes out onto the sidewalk from the clothing boutique in the next building. Relief warms me when I open the heavy door to the coffee shop and see that there's no line. I focus on the task at hand and my breaths. While I wait behind a short man wearing overalls who fidgets annoyingly with his keys, I focus on the smell of coffee and cinnamon in the air, which remind me of Josephine and her office, it always smells a little like a coffee shop thanks to her Starbucks habit (similar to mine). Way back when I was seeing Josephine regularly, she taught me about mindfulness. Focus on the exact moment you are in. I make it through the wait, place my order, and then head back without a panic attack.

I don't need to be buzzed into the office because I have a key. When I push open the door to the office I hear:

"...she's terrified and doesn't want to be alone."

I stay in the doorway alone, where they can't see me.

"Bernice, you gotta get her back to school. God, what will she do if she doesn't graduate? A young beautiful girl with everything. Really is such a shame."

Now I push the door all the way open. "I brought treats," I say brightly. I place the scones and coffee on the table and although my heart pounds, I look Eleanor in the eye and say, "Did Mom tell you I'm writing a book for my senior project? I need to nail the scene where the girl has a nervous breakdown before she graduates. Ticking clock and all that," I say and wink. I smile at my mother and duck into the other room and resume breathing.

.   .   .   .   .

I drop some more Rescue Remedy into my mouth because my heart is pounding. I put the little bottle back into my pocket and open my laptop and turn it on. I stare at the desktop, which is a picture of me, Susan, and Peter from the summer. Tan and smiling.

I click open a browser and check my email. I have fifty unread messages. Without reading who they are from, I highlight the entire group and press delete. Then I go into my trash and select empty trash. I skim over the only chapter I have written way back before The Episode then take out my notes and outline and read through it.

Mom pops her head in about an hour later.

"Honey, I'm so sorry about Eleanor."

I shake my head without looking up. "No, no. It's fine. I mean, you know if I can't make the college thing happen, there's always modeling."

We laugh.

I reread a sentence from my outline that says: "California was the only answer. College was not."

Mom walks all the way in. "It's good to see you working on your book."

I nod and continue to reread those words, thinking about Dr. Foster and about how I wrote this long before my panic attack. "Watch it," I whisper to myself, "If you're not careful, you'll fall headlong into another one." Breathe, one, two, three.

Mom leans on the table, her manicured nails bare of the usual soft pink polish. Her diamond ring looks a little dirty. I wonder what else she has neglected since I went crazy.

"Your teachers know what's going on. Even Mrs. Dubois said that you can have an extension for the book." She touches my hair lightly.

A lump forms in my throat, but I can't pinpoint what's making me want to cry.

Mom takes a deep breath.

I nod without looking at her. The sound of me rustling papers fills the room.

Then Mom hugs me tight.

CHAPTER EIGHT
HITTING BOTTOM

Wednesday morning, I wake up early. I'm too afraid to go for a run even though I want to. Instead I take to the treadmill in the basement and when I come back upstairs, Mom is just waking up, putting the coffee beans into the grinder. She smiles sleepily. "Good to see you running, honey."

I don't want to stay for small talk because I'm on a kind of adrenalin high and have convinced myself that I should go back up to my room to write chapter 2, a new addition to the outline of my book, called The Breakdown. I just nod and begin to walk through the kitchen.

"Barb and Cliff are coming over for brunch today. They don't have to work until later, and I'm taking the morning off. Now that we know Bubbie is fine, time to move on to Barb and time to meet this fellow." Tingles of panic flutter in the base of my spine, but I refuse to lose my mojo, so I say, "Oh, that's good." And continue the journey back to my room. I can't stop now.

•   •   •   •   •

I've taken a quick shower and am sitting at my desk staring at the outline again. I crumple it up. Forget "The Breakdown." This is, after all supposed to be fiction. The answer comes to me: The chapter 1 I wrote before will be the prologue. Starting from there, I open my laptop and wait for it to come to life. Then I pull up a blank Word doc. On the top, I type in all caps: PREMISE and continue with:

Minutes after high school graduation, "Mya" takes off to California to reconnect with the only boy she's ever loved, "Dylan", who was sent away to rehab after an overdose the year before.

I pause and then type: CHAPTER 1 SUMMARY.

"Mya" packs her bags in the middle of the night, rolls her car down the driveway so no one hears her leave, and heads out of "Littleville." On her way she calls her two best friends, Holden and Phoebe, for advice about what to say when she arrives at the rehab center.

I stop again. Holden and Phoebe. Can I ever stop being obsessed with *Catcher in the Rye*? Problem is figuring out if "Dylan" knows she's coming to California. Does she call him? Does she even have his number? Ah. This is what I HATE about writing. All the details. All the little things that explain the motivation. I just want to write their first kiss scene which I can't help but picture against the brick building of the rehab and that's because one of my early make-out sessions with Justin was against a tree. It was a kiss that changed everything. I look at the bulletin board next to my computer and see the senior project handouts. Mrs. Dubois connected me with a local author to help me with writing. I see her name—Alyssa Yoo—and email address handwritten at the top of one of the sheets. Maybe it's time to email her. I quickly minimize my documents and pull up a web browser. I click into my email and type a short email to her. I hit send and take a deep breath. My chest is tight. How will I ever write an entire book by the end of the school year?

The wind blows my hair and I curse my old Toyota. A week-long drive across the country minus a/c is going to suck. I reach for my earpiece and call Holden first.

"I so wish I could come with you," he says as soon as he answers, knowing full well that I'm already in the car, even though it's 3 a.m.

"Me too," I sigh and look out the windshield at the starless sky. "Listen, I'm freaking out about seeing Dylan. It's been a year. He has no idea I'm coming. What do I say to him?"

"You have the whole ride to think about that..."

I stop typing and stare at the black on white in front of me. I'm totally plot-dumping and my dialogue sounds like some dumb soap opera. I press delete until every black letter is gone. It's the third time I've done this in the last twenty minutes. I hear Mrs. Dubois in my head: "Writer's block is about inaction. Even if everything you write is crap, you are writing and therefore not blocked. Write through the block. Keep at it."

I begin to type again. I see that airhead idiot client of Mom's Eleanor, her veneers shimmering and her finger pointing at me.

I have to keep going.

Which I do. For another two hours. I only come up with four pages because I type and delete a lot for the first hour. When I look at the clock, it's 10 o'clock. I check my email to see if that author responded. Not yet.

Time for brunch.

.   .   .   .   .

"Hello?"

I hear my sister's voice and the chest tightness returns and a little behind the ear burning to top it off. But I push the feelings away best I can and return Barb's greeting.

"Hi!" I yell and continue to slice mushrooms for Mom.

"We're all in the kitchen," Mom calls, taking out an oversized frying pan and putting it on the stovetop.

I hear the shuffling of multiple foots steps and scoop all the mushrooms up with two hands.

They stand in the kitchen. Grinning. I freeze, holding the mushrooms. Barb has never looked tinier in her life standing next to Cliff who is a large black man with long dreadlocks and glasses. He's holding a bunch of flowers in one hand and Barb's in another.

The clink of metal on metal and the hum of the fridge disappear for several static moments. If someone took a picture, you would be able to clearly see my parents' surprise, but it's a quick passing expression for them both because the still moment ends and the noises in the kitchen all begin again.

"Hi, I'm Cliff." He lets go of Barb's hand and reaches for my father's.

"Hello, nice to meet you, Cliff." Dad gives his hand a few quick pumps.

"Hello, I'm Bernice." Mom wipes her hands on her apron, and then Cliff's hand swallows hers. They both grin awkwardly at each other.

My turn. I smile, dump the mushrooms in the pan and introduce myself.

There's another stillness but Cliff breaks it. "I hear you make amazing omelets, Bernice? I'm a cook myself. Can I help?"

And that's all it takes. Cliff and Mom whip up veggie omelets topped with chives picked from Mom's garden and freshly squeezed orange juice. Dad makes more coffee. The three of them chat about food. I hang back and put dishes into the dishwasher and wipe counter tops. Barb is smiling a lot and quiet, watching our parents talk to Cliff. Then Barb takes my hand and brings me into the dining room.

"Isn't he great?" She opens the china cabinet and whispers to me.

I don't know what to say other than, "He looked pretty professional chopping those chives." I pull out a stack of dishes.

She takes the plates from me and begins to put them out on the table. "Cliff was a cop but was let go when he was caught buying drugs. That was ten years ago. Then he went back to cooking school. He's been head chef at this fancy, Italian restaurant in Westport on the waterfront."

"Wait. How old is he?" He didn't strike me as particularly old but doing the math...

She doesn't stop what she's doing or look at me. She's moved onto putting out the good silverware and napkins. Things clink and clank onto the table.

"Barb, how old is Cliff?" My voice is a loud whisper.

She stops finally because there's nothing else to put out except glasses, which are underneath the china cabinet.

"He's forty."

"Forty!"

She pushes past me and opens the bottom doors of the china cabinet. "What?"

"Barb, that's pretty old."

"It's only fourteen years."

She hands me some glasses. We look at each other.

"What?"

"He's also a former drug addict?"

"Maddie, don't start with me. I've been sober for the last year, no relapse and he has about ten years in, so don't lecture me."

We put the glasses out in silence. One almost slips out of my hand, but I catch it before anybody notices. Except now I can barely breathe. Her I go, panicking. And I'm worried about Barb? What's that old saying about glass houses and throwing stones?

Finally, the glasses are done, and we have no choice but to go back in but before we do I grab her arm. "I'm just worried. With Michael gone—"

Her eyes flash and her mouth trembles a little. "Michael, contrary to what you may think, never kept me sober. I did."

I open my mouth, but she puts her face close to me, more like to my neck because she's so much shorter than me. "You need to get a life, Maddie. Stop worrying about me. Looks like you have enough to worry about on your own."

"Yeah, I already thought of that."

"Good thing you're taller than me," Barb said.

"Why's that?" I ask, glowering down at her.

" 'Cuz you wouldn't be able to cop an attitude looking up my nose."

"Maybe now," I bluster. "Maybe now I actually might have time to get a life, since you so obviously don't need me anymore."

She rolls her eyes and opens her mouth to retort but instead shakes her head then walks back into the kitchen.

.   .   .   .   .

My adrenalin high is gone and taken over by a post-brunch hangover (pun intended). I was silent during breakfast and didn't pay much attention to the conversation. Cliff looked my way a lot and smiled.

"I like your glasses," I offer. "Uh, very retro."

He just smiles back at me.

Everyone is in the living room, but it might as well just be Cliff and Mom. They have moved from what's the best brand of knives to crème fraiche or milk for scrambled eggs and do you beat them with a whisk or a fork. Barb beams and Dad looks pretty happy. So, what's wrong with me?

Disconnected. Everyone is moving on in their lives. But me.

· · · · ·

As they leave, Barb grabs me into a tight hug and whispers, "I love you, Maddie." Mom, Dad, and Cliff hug too. Then Cliff turns to me and I'm kind of over the whole hugging thing, so I stick my hand out, "Nice to meet you Cliff." He looks disappointed but pumps my arm in a hearty shake. It's cold by the doorway so my parents are already gone by this point. I just want to crawl back to bed but before I can Barb says, "Walk us to the car?"

"I don't have a jacket," I protest.

Cliff shrugs off his enormous leather bomber jacket and puts it around me.

"Walk with us," he orders.

We step out into the bitter cold sunshine. I follow behind them down the steps and across the driveway. When we reach their car, Cliff turns to me. Barb huddles next to him.

"Maddie, I know we don't know each other well. But B's told me about what you've been going through." He takes his glasses off and rubs his eyes and his dreadlocks swish a little back and forth.

I feel myself get hot and I shoot good ole "B" a look.

But Cliff apparently doesn't let anything slide because he puts his glasses back on and says, "Hey, now. Don't get mad at your sis. That woman loves you more than you will ever know. Listen to me, because like your sis, I've been through total hell and I— both of us—have hit the dirty bottom."

The heat inside me bypasses anxiety and goes straight to anger. "I don't drink or do drugs, Cliff. I don't have a 'bottom'." I put air quotes around the word. "Dirty or otherwise."

He gives a hearty laugh and throws a knowing look at my sis B (makes me want to puke). "Everyone, little sis, has a bottom."

I cross my arms. "I'm not and never will be your 'little sis'."

"Maddie," Barb or, excuse me, B, gives me a nudge in my shoulder. I shake her off and glare at Cliff who smiles in that way that condescending adults do to kids when they are thinking *oh she thinks she knows everything, just wait...*

"Listen, Maddie. I'm telling you that everyone has a bottom and you seem to be hitting yours. Do you know what happens next? I mean you should. You've seen B here a few times at the bottom."

God, she has told him everything.

"What happens, Maddie, after you hit bottom?" Barb asks me softly with tears in the corner of her eyes.

I shake my head because I don't want to open my mouth because now all of the sudden, out of nowhere, tears clump in my throat. My bottom is rising to the top. And I hate it. Almost as much as jelly doughnuts.

Cliff leans down so we are almost face-to-face. I refuse to tilt my head to look at him. "You look up. Maddie, once you reach that bottom, that's it. Then you have no choice but to look up."

I don't move or say anything.

.   .   .   .   .

After everyone is gone and I take a brief nap, I'm at the computer checking my email. Alyssa Yoo is in my inbox. I do the happy dance and click it open:

Dear Maddie, I'm happy to take a look at your work for your senior project. In fact, maybe we can set up a schedule to follow? Let me know the details about deadlines and such, and then we can create a writing and feedback schedule for your work. Mrs. Dubois has told me about the work you've done for the literary magazine and school newspaper (she sent me one of your stories "The Ticking Boy" about the girl who falls for a boy with Tourette's. What a touching piece!). Anyway, I'm excited you contacted me, and looking forward to working together!

Best, Alyssa Yoo

I'm smiling so hard my lips tingle. I email her back with the deadline date of the rough draft and final draft. I attach all the other paperwork that Mrs. Dubois emailed to all the seniors in September.

I'm looking up.

Chapter Nine
Back to Life

The whole rest of the week I focused on writing and running on the treadmill every day. At night, Bubbie and I checked in with each other and gave each other pep talks. I tried little trips to the supermarket (not driving, just tagging along) and drug store. By the weekend, my parents didn't even have to ask. I was going back to school. It's the perfect week to do it. Just three days to Thanksgiving.

Sunday night I lay out my back to school outfit—jeans and a turtleneck sweater—and take a long hot shower before bed. It's been a good day. I went for a run on the treadmill and wrote almost thirty pages of my book. They may not be the greatest pages, but I'm writing. I even replied to Alyssa and sent her all thirty pages.

In the morning, I get up and dress quickly. My mother hands me my lunch and a travel mug of tea. My father drives me to school and says he would pick me up right at 1:40. None of us are comfortable with me driving yet.

Peter and Susan meet me in the lobby and then hustle me down to the senior corridor. "You have to get back into your life, Maddie." Susan says as we stop at my locker.

"Yeah and we are here, and you will let us help you." Peter does his stern father routine and waits patiently as I turn the lock of my locker.

"It's not that bad, guys," I tell them and rub the bottle of Rescue Remedy in my pocket.

I leave them to meet with Mrs. Dubois, and we decide my duties as school newspaper editor will be taken over by the girl who will become editor next year, a fresh-faced junior who has buck teeth and very straight hair. She has no personality but knows more about independent and dependent clauses than Mrs. Dubois.

Every move is robotic. I hurry on stiff legs back down to Mrs. Dubois and sit in class and listen to her talk about Odysseus' return to Ithaca after the Trojan War. His wife and son thought he was dead. He returns after ten years, and it is not the sweet homecoming he wished and thought it would be. As I watch Mrs. Dubois scribbling all kinds of notes on the chalkboard—none of which I write down—I daydream of a similar type homecoming after going away to college. I come home to my room transformed into a pink and frilly gift-wrapping room for Mom. Peter and Susan send me emails saying they are taking semesters abroad or saving the whales or something, and they aren't returning home.

My heart pounds. My chest tightens.

I look at the clock and see class has just begun. I do what Mrs. Dubois had instructed me to do during our brief chat this morning. "Just get up and go, if you have to. No big deal."

I slide out the back door of the classroom. No one even looks over when my chair scrapes against the floor.

My heart slows down as soon as my clogs hit the linoleum. I don't have a hall pass. The smell of breakfast is still in the air mixed with some kind of cleaner. I feel my jeans pocket. Cell phone. Check. Rescue Remedy. Check.

My heart steadies. I go to the sink and splash water on my face. Then I go into one of the stalls. When I finish, I stand up in mountain pose and do some breathing. Gotta get through the day. Don't want to disappoint my parents or Susan and Peter.

I feel my phone vibrate in my jeans. I pull it out and look at the screen but don't recognize it. Must be a wrong number. I stuff it back into my pocket and take another deep breath and go back to class.

·   ·   ·   ·   ·

"You made it!"

We stand together outside of school. It's sunny and warmer than it should be. Peter puts his arm around me and squeezes.

"It wasn't that hard." I lie.

"Really?" Susan loops an arm through mine.

"I'm fine. I got through it."

I lean against the stonewall that's in front of the entrance to school. I know my dad will be a little late.

"Let us take you home," Peter says as he pulls out his shades.

"Yeah, maybe we can go for coffee?" Susan says.

I watch Peter clean his glasses and make his irritated noise like when he orders a bagel and it has poppy seeds on it.

Susan narrows her eyes at me.

A year from now we won't be doing this.

"Maddie?"

"Hey? Do you want to sit down?"

"I'm fine." I cross my arms and shift my weight. I want to go home and crawl under the covers.

Susan and Peter hover closer to me.

"When was the last time you went for a run *outside*??"

I don't respond to Susan

"Why don't we all go home and go for a run around the neighborhood together?"

Now I laugh. Susan is as athletic as Peter. Neither do more than exercise their enormous brains. Peter lifts weights a little and uses his parents' home gym. But Susan? Ha! She takes classes here and there. She follows the trends. This month it's—

"...belly-dancing class with me tonight?"

Now I have to join in. "Peter, you up for that?"

He throws me a dirty look. "Oh, 'cause I'm gay?"

We all laugh.

As we giggle and Susan belly dances for us I hear, "Madeline?" I look out into the parking lot and see—

This is not happening...*again*? Sean? Really? He has this way of always just *appearing*.

My heart pounds but not in an anxiety way. Peter and Susan's voices fade away. Then, way too loud and clear, I hear, "Hey, sweetie. Sorry I'm so late."

There's my dad with his crazy hair sticking out of the window of his car. "Oh, Dad... "

Sean leans out of his window and waves at me.

I look from my dad back to Sean. "Hang on a second," I tell him.

I run to my dad's car. "Dad," I'm out of breath. "Is it okay if I go home with Susan and Peter?" I don't know why I don't just tell him about Sean.

He looks past me to Susan and Peter who get that invisible signal I send off and come to car. "We have a project for AP English, Mr. Hickman. I can drive Maddie home."

"Oh, well." His face says relief. He thinks this means I'm back to normal. "School was good then?"

"Yeah, it was good." I push my lips into a full smile.

"Good. Peter, just have her home in time for dinner. You two can stay if you want? Mrs. Hickman is making lasagna."

My awesome best friends both shake their heads.

"Gotta work on my senior project," Peter says.

"I have an AP Chem test tomorrow." Susan is as believable as Peter.

"Another time. Have a good time with your project, kids."

We wave to my father as he leaves. As soon as he is out of sight, I turn back to Sean and see him hanging out the window smiling. Susan and Peter each hug me. "Go have a fun afternoon," Peter whispers in my ear.

I nod and say back, "I will."

.   .   .   .   .

I click my seatbelt in and say to Sean, "You seem to have a way of just showing up."

"Is that bad?"

"No...kind of supernatural. Just when I'm feeling really shitty, you pop up and all the stress fades away."

"Glad I can be of service."

We drive down the long driveway out of school.

"Why so shitty?"

"Just a lot of stuff going on…" I want to tell him that this was my first day back to school since I lost my mind, but this time around I will opt for withholding…a little.

"Family?"

Easy way out, so I nod.

The car slows to a stop. Cars are bumper to bumper as we approach the exit.

I reach for something in my mind to talk about that's not too crazy. So, I blurt out, "I'm writing a book. For senior project."

"Really?

"Yeah, it's fun." I'm so lame. *Fun?*

He laughs. "You say that like it's skiing or something."

I laugh.

"Now my senior year, I totally coasted. Thought I knew it all." He glances at me. "You don't seem to be coasting with writing a book and everything."

"I'm doing okay." I nibble on my cuticle. "Actually, writing the book is kind of cathartic." I stop not wanting to ruin this non-date date with my rambling.

He clicks on his turn signal. He looks left and then right. "I didn't freak out until I got to college. First semester. Total break down."

I watch his hands turn the wheel, trying to find the right way to react and wanting to scream, "Yay! Someone else *not* over forty knows what this feels like!"

Instead I ask, "What happened?"

He drives with one hand on the bottom of the wheel and the other on the shift in the middle console. "I went to UVM for the first year as a physics major, thinking it was a more practical idea than theater. I flunked everything. Went home at Christmas and crawled into bed for a month. Actually, cried when my parents said I had to go back."

"But you went back?"

"Yep. Because I am always and forever, the best son. Didn't want to burden them with my misery. But I decided that I wasn't going to stay a physics major. Second semester I switched majors to theater and general science and reapplied to schools closer to home and now—"

"Here you are."

"Here I am."

He asks where to go and the only place I can think of is Starbucks. Perfect for a non-date date. We drive along. The heater fills the air between us.

Then he says, "I called you."

"When?"

"Today. I know I should have called you before, like right after we saw each other. I hope you weren't mad. I thought you might be because you didn't call me, but then I was thinking you could be waiting for me to call you."

Maybe I should tell him about my own mental melt down. But I opt for: "Actually, I don't have your number in my phone." Which is true.

I pull my phone out and look at the last number that had come up when I was in the bathroom. I read it to him.

"Yep," He grins. "That was me."

I highlight it and click 'add to contacts'. "It's official. You're in my phone."

"It's official."

We pull into Starbucks and as we get out of the car I ask, "Any tips on avoiding a 'total melt down'?"

CHAPTER TEN
CATCH UP

"Catch me up? When we talked on the phone last week you said you'd seen Dr. Foster."

"Twice," I hold up two fingers for proof.

Josephine smiles. "Twice. And you returned to school?"

"It's been two weeks. A week and a half because of Thanksgiving."

"And you're on some medicine." She glances down at her pad of paper where a bunch of scribbles take up most of the page.

"Yeah, I've taken it just a few times when I was having a full panic attack. I took the SATs this Saturday and took it then. But I rely on this—" I pull out my Rescue Remedy.

Josephine laughs and reaches down into her purse resting by her feet. "Me, too."

"Should I be worried that my shrink is popping the same meds as me?"

Josephine shakes her head. "No, you should be glad. That's why I can do what I do."

Sufficiently warmed up, we get right into it. I relay all the events of the last few weeks. She listens as she usually does. Her hands folded in her lap and her head cocked to the side. Nodding and mmhhmmming to let me know she's listening.

"When I get panicked I just do the stuff you've taught me, or if it's really bad, like I said, I know I have the meds. And sometimes just knowing I have it makes me calm down." I pull my legs up and sit cross-legged on the couch. "And, Dr. Foster says I only need to come back to check in about every month or so. But he also said that if I'm seeing you, I don't have to continue with him."

"Are you seeing me?"

"Yes. Yes. I'd like to see you."

"Weekly?"

Even though I nod, the panic crackles through.

She cocks her head. "Will that work for you?"

"Yeah," but my voice is a little weak.

"What are you thinking?"

"I don't know," I whisper.

We sit silently, just the faint click of the small clock on the table next to me. I know what she wants me to do right now because I know how she rolls in moments like this.

"I guess," I search for words or thoughts, but everything is kind of blank. "I guess I'm afraid."

"Of?"

My mind fills now with just these far away images of me in a cap and gown, of me driving away from home. It makes my heart pound.

"Leaving." I say it and can't believe how true it is.

"That's pretty normal, Maddie. Going away to college for the first time is a major milestone."

"I know but it's definitely hitting me harder than my friends."

"Maybe. But you don't know because it's not something that you all are going to talk about necessarily." She pushes a stray, short, black strand of hair out of her face. "Tell me about now. What's going on right now in your life? Focusing on the now will help you not feel so anxious about the future."

And, of course, she's right because I tell her all about Sean and instead of my heart pounding in fear, it pounds with excitement.

When I leave and get into my car—I started driving myself over the weekend— I check my phone and see that Sean called. This is where I will be from now on, in the present. Not the past and not the future—no matter how scared I am.

．　．　　．　．　　．

And when I check my email that night, it's from Alyssa and proves to be the message/sign that I can and will move forward, that I can leave my fears behind.

Dear Maddie,

I read your pages last night and wanted to respond to you as my thoughts are fresh. In a nutshell, I want to say that I'm impressed. Your dialogue and the voice of Mya are spot on and your writing is clear and honest. What's most impressive is the way you seem to be able to portray Dylan even though the story is in first person and, therefore, limited in perspective. But you use that dialogue and the contrast between the two characters (their differences, oy vey!) in relating to the world around them. Really splendid job. Despite his bad boyness, despite all the pain these two have caused each other, it's clear that they have a deep connection and an unstoppable electrical charge between them...I'm definitely rooting for their success.

And that's why I feel that I can push you harder than most of the high school students I have mentored. I think we are beyond tense issues or maintaining a consistent point of view. Clearly you are a reader because you are mastering the art of writing the novel and only good readers who read like a writer can do that. I want to recommend a list of craft books for you.

Attached are my notes. I'm not gonna lie, there's a lot of suggestions for revision but you are up to the challenge.

I think that you already know you are a good writer. Now I want you to prove to yourself that you can write an amazing novel.

Looking forward,

Alyssa

Amazing novel. Maybe. I'd settle for a novel. Completed. I hit print on Alyssa's notes. I'm up for the challenge.

CHAPTER ELEVEN
ESCAPE

Sean makes keeping my promise to stay "in the moment" easy. Since I saw him on that Monday about three weeks ago we have talked every night, and he has picked me up from school a few more times. But tonight, we went to dinner and now we're here at the overlook at the edge of the woods in town.

We pull up to the low fence and the view is all lights and stars. In front of us is a clearing, and we can see the deep black sky and the little flickers of light from the stars.

The heat blasts in Sean's car, a sound like the white noise machine in Dr. Foster's office waiting room. Behind us are the woods. A place where kids from all the neighboring towns tumble into to have a bonfire and a smoke. A place where the police crawl from Friday sundown to Sunday sun up. But tonight is the big basketball game between our town and our biggest rival, so not another car in sight.

We talk about our day. I tell him about the A plus I got on my *Odysseus* paper, that I already finished the edits for Alyssa and have written another ten pages.

"I want to read this masterpiece."

Not if you knew it was all about my ex-boyfriend. The fantasy happy ending I wish I had with my ex-boyfriend. "Not yet," I say and look out the window at the flickering.

"Writing is the only thing that helps me escape—" I want to say, 'my life now', but instead I say, "my stress. Makes me lose the moment, forget everything."

"That's why I like to act. To escape." And then he adds, shyly: "Lately being with you, it's almost better than acting."

I can see out of the corner of my eye, he's looking at me. He reaches for my hand, which is a little shaky but when I look at it, it's fine. His hand is soft and warm. Mine is clammy. I'm with Sean. This is real. This could be better than any story I write about Justin. If I just try, a little.

"I really like you." He runs his thumb over mine. "Don't think I ever stopped."

His words make me squirm a little, so I say:

"Let's go outside, out there. To the woods. There's a little stream somewhere in there."

"It's cold—"

But I'm out the door already and running towards the woods. I remember running back there with Justin and hopping on some stepping-stones that seemed perfectly placed across the stream.

I slow down and turn and run backwards, waving Sean towards me. I drop my jacket and feel the wind through my cords. I pull up the turtleneck to cover my chin and mouth as I run. My boots crunch over the cold ground. Sean picks up my jacket, laughing.

"Be careful!" He calls to me. "It's dark out here. Hey, slow down!"

I stop in front of an old gnarled tree. There's a tree in my yard that's smaller version of this one, with branches that are perfect reclining seats. I want to climb this one. I put a hand on it and then hoist myself with my foot secured onto a low branch. My foot slips.

"Ow!"

Sean swoops down, and I feel myself being lifted. His face is inches from mine.

I wince. "My butt."

"Should I rub it?" He's half-kidding.

I decide to try and be sexy, but instead I squeak awkwardly, "Yes."

He puts me down gently and leans himself against the tree carefully, covering my butt with one hand. Then he pulls me by my hips towards him. A flicker of the memory of my first kiss with Justin passes through my mind, but I put my hands on either side of Sean's cold face and the memory fades. The only light is from the moon that falls between the thick trees. I pull Sean's face to mine and let my cold nose touch his. Then our foreheads touch. He smells like breath mints.

Our mouths are open when they touch. We keep kissing and I think of nothing but the cold air against my back and the warmth and softness of Sean's lips. He kneads my butt. It doesn't hurt anymore. When he guides me to the ground and pulls me on top of him, I still only think of kissing him and the cold air.

．　　　．　　　．　　　．　　　．

Sean kisses my neck and I see my jacket next to me, his is under my head like a pillow.

"Are you alright?" He whispers into my neck.

"Yes," I breathe into his.

His hands move from under my turtleneck to the top of my jeans. "Is this okay?"

I feel dizzy lying on the ground.

"Yes," I say again.

Sean kisses my neck again. I squeeze my eyes shut and try to relax, but my legs feel shaky. I wait to feel something. I don't know what I'm supposed to feel, so I reach for his zipper.

Everything kinds of stops when my hand touches his boxers.

"You're not alright," he says. "I can tell."

"Come back. I'm fine."

"Maybe I rushed this. I just got caught up." He looks up at the sky and then back to me. "We don't have to do anything, you know."

"I—" The air pierces my throat. I can taste the cold.

"I hope you don't think this is all I want." He zips his pants.

"No!"

"Because if that's what you think of me..."

I reach out for his hand. I still feel dizzy.

"No!"

"Because, you know, if I just wanted a hand job—"

"Sean."

He sits back on his heels. "Let's go." He sighs. "It's getting late. I promised your Dad you'd be home by eleven-thirty."

I fix my pants and shirt. When I'm done I say, "This has nothing to do with you." I reach for his arm. The moon is farther away, smaller and dimmer.

He shrugs me off him, but gently, and stands up.

"Listen," I stand, too. "I haven't...you know... I haven't had anyone... you know, do *that.*"

But he doesn't say anything back just reaches down and grabs our jackets. Then he puts my jacket over my shoulders and finally says, "I just felt you tense up." He balls up his own jacket and stuffs it under his arm. "I guess I'm waiting for you to say, 'Forget it. I just like you like a brother.'"

"I can assure you that there's no brotherly-sisterly feelings on this end."

"Good." He puts an arm around me, and we walk silently to the car.

"Never?" He stops at the car. "Not with Justin or Zak?"

I shake my head.

He opens the car door for me. "You didn't want to?"

"This is embarrassing!" I slide into the front seat. When he gets in and shuts his door I say, "But if you must know...With Justin, he was drunk when he tried the first time, and then we pretty much fell apart shortly after. With Zak...I liked him, but as far as being really attracted to him, like in a way that would make me physically want to—" I can't find the right words and the only words that come to me sound like health class or something.

"He didn't turn you on?"

I giggle, which makes him giggle.

"Are we really talking about this?" He says.

"At least we're talking. Maybe next time I'll relax."

"Yeah," he sighs, but he's smiling. "Me, too."

.   .   .   .   .

"I can't believe that Boy Scout Sean actually said the words 'hand job'." Susan slaps the table and nudges Peter.

"Jesus, I can't even say—" He looks at us, red faced. "I can't even say—"

he stops again and looks around and then whispers, "*Hand job* and I'm a guy!"

I take a sip of my decaf latte. "He said it, and sadly, I didn't do it."

Susan raises a pierced eyebrow, "Sadly? You wanted to?"

I mull this a bit, cupping my hands around the warm mug. "Not because it was such a turn on or anything but more because isn't it kind of time for me to move to that stage?"

"What?" Both Susan and Peter look confused.

"See my shrinks—" God, it really is a plural thing. "Seem to believe that I, on some level, don't want to fully grow up. Isn't sex or, you know," I lower my voice, "hand jobs kind of a more advanced level of a relationship?"

Susan slaps the table again and my latte, Peter's tea, and her hot cocoa shake. "Anyone can give a hand job." She motions with her hand, but Peter catches it expertly as if catching a baseball before it falls to the ground.

"Listen," Peter shoots a nasty look at Susan like she is a heathen. "The deal with this is that if you like someone, you want to take it to the next level because you want to make them feel good and vice versa. Don't do it to grow up."

I sip my latte again and look around the coffee shop. None of my favorite baristas are here. It looks like a whole new crew. My chest hurts.

"It's been a long time since we've come here for coffee."

"Are you changing the subject because you are embarrassed or because you don't know what to say?"

"I don't know. Maybe both. But seriously, no more Barista Bob." We all turn to the drink bar and see lots of intelligent looking, hipster guys and girls, none familiar to us.

"Let's forget this whole hand job thing for a minute." Susan taps her empty cup against the table. "What I want to know is have you been able to forget about Justin. You haven't said anything about him since you got together with Sean."

That's because I've immersed myself in the "now," in the present. In Sean. In school. I don't say this because then I'd have to explain it, and since I don't fully understand how I'm doing that, I just say, "He's kind of left my mind. The panic stuff and everything sort of pushed it—I guess the past—

all away." Except late at night when I can't fall asleep. I fantasize about Justin and I getting together again…Somehow, some way. Or, I think about my story, "Mya" reuniting with "Dylan", the current scene I've been trying to write. She shows up at his rehab and has to argue with the secretary to get in…All that tension leading up to when they first kiss again, in the room he shares with this older guy/Jesus looking type… But I don't say any of this out loud.

"All I know is that it's senior year bitches! And whatever way we want to get through it, we go for it. Peter's got Jack. You've got Sean. And I've got me. Yes friends, I'm dedicating the rest of the year to fabulous me. So, when you all go off on your dates and stuff, don't fret over me. I'm busy loving myself!"

Peter and I look at each other and burst out laughing.

"What?" She says her face completely not kidding. "I'm serious."

"I know," Peter says putting an arm around her and kissing the top of her head. "I know."

CHAPTER TWELVE
BLAST FROM THE PAST

After Susan and Peter drop me off at home, I check my email before working a little on my book. Sean is going to be away all of next weekend for a theater competition and I promised him a few pages to read in the car on the way. I'm about to hit send on a scene where Mya flashes back to being a little kid with Phoebe, Holden, and Dylan, and Dylan tries to kiss her on the playground when my inbox chimes. An unfamiliar address pops up: jno@hotmail.com and of course the letter J, as it always does when I see it written or typed, makes my heart skip. I don't know Justin's email address. Could it be?

Maddie,

I'm might give up after this email. I sent you two other ones in November. Maybe your address has changed. I'm going to try one more time. Hope it's the charm. :)

It's been way too long since we have talked.

Zak would be a junior now and Mia would have been a sophomore in college. Do you think about Zak a lot? I hate to say it, but I don't think of Mia as often.

NOAH JACOBS?!

But I do think about you.

I'm going to be visiting Columbia this weekend and thought maybe we could meet for coffee or something. I know it's kind of last minute, only because you didn't respond to my other emails : (

I understand if you can't do it, but it would be cool to see you.

Noah.

Maybe this is even better than Justin. I so should have checked some of those emails I deleted back during the insane asylum time.

"But I do think of you."

Noah. Beautiful Noah. Sweet Noah. Parallel lives Noah. He was another CIT from camp that summer I was with Zak. I have thought about Noah so many times, replaying the gentle no-tongue-but-I-wanted-it kiss we shared before we went back home.

Noah. He lost his girlfriend just months before camp to a drunk driver. When Zak was killed, it was Noah who helped me find a way to stay at camp, to attend the memorial service that the camp had for him. But then once we left, we only emailed a few times and then it just stopped.

All I know is I'm glad Sean has to be away this weekend because I really want to see Noah again.

.   .   .   .   .

I linger in the entrance to Starbuck's on Broadway, which is hard to do because people are coming in and going out quickly. I see Noah through the crowd, but he can't see me. He sits in the corner against one of the tall windows. His hair still golden brown but much longer. His head is bent over the *Wall Street Journal,* which I kind of find lame. I would expect *The Voice* or the *Times*.

I finally move out of the doorway and make my way through the crowd of college students dressed in jeans and thick sweaters and professor-types in khakis and dress shirts.

"Noah?"

He looks up and a lock of dark honey brown hair flops in front of his eyes, I just want to grab him into a tight hug.

"Maddie!" He pushes his chair back and almost bumps into the single skinny man clutching a latte in one hand and a cell phone in the other. "Sorry." Noah turns back to me and finishes standing all the way up.

He's definitely at least a good four inches taller than me. I know we weren't that far apart two years ago. He bends down and hugs me. I smell sunshine and fresh air.

I slide a chair out and sit down. "You're all grown up!" How witty. How mature.

He laughs. "Tell me all about you, what's going on? How have you been?"

I fiddle with a straw rapper and try to find a good opening. "Aside from some senior year stress, things have been okay." I stop fiddling. "Actually, I'm writing a book for my senior project."

"Really! Man, I haven't written anything other than essays for school since camp." He smiles crookedly. "I've been kind of stressed too with college stuff. Hey, do you want a drink?"

"Yeah," I reach for my purse on the table.

"Since I made you schlep from Connecticut to the City, let me get it." He puts his hand on top of mine, which is still on the purse. "You used to like coffee with lots of sugar and cream. Should I get that?"

I can barely reply because I'm super-aware of his hand.

I nod and then correct myself. "Decaf."

"Really?"

"Yeah, I'll fill you in. There's a whole song and dance about it."

The rest of the afternoon slips away as we sit and relive each other's last two years. The sun moves from one side of Starbuck's to the other and the café empties out and fills back up. I told my parents I would be home late. They seemed relieved that I was willing to travel so far by myself. I have my Rescue Remedy and anxiety pills, so I feel equipped.

I fill Noah in about the panic and his response: "I've been on Zoloft since Mia died."

We sit back in our chairs. The voices around us are kind of like background music. I feel incredibly relaxed, each muscle releases. He looks one way, towards the coffee bar, and I look the other, out the window. I see a guy with an African print shirt walking by, holding a set of bongos. Then a tall black-haired woman wrapped up in a shawl, strides by, like a model, holding a Zabar's bag.

"Hey, are you getting hungry?" Noah asks.

I nod, thinking of that Zabar's bag. I love going to Zabar's. You can get an entire meal there.

"I know what we can do for dinner."

"Sure. Are we dressed for it?"

"Oh, there's no dress code. And we don't eat there." I grab my purse. "If you're going to live in the City, you have to experience Zabar's."

We shrug on our jackets and leave Starbuck's. I pretend to be a tour guide and lead the way to Zabar's, which is just down Broadway but about a half hour walk. His eyes get big when we walk in. Zabar's knishes and H & H hot bagels are my favorite parts of the City. Forget all the Broadway shows and shopping and even the restaurants. It's the little things you can't get in the suburbs that make the City the City.

"I want to buy everything!" Noah says as he scans the walls of food. We reach the cold cuts and cheese section "Fresh mozzarella!"

We spend over a half hour loading up on too much food. A smorgasbord of Jewish and Italian treats. Noah grabs a tomato and mozzarella salad and carved turkey and cranberry sandwich. I put minestrone soup and crusty bread in the basket. We both dive for the vegetarian sushi rolls at the same time.

"I think I know what school I'm going to." We laugh.

"Good reason to choose a school. Forget the Ivy League thing."

"Yeah, Ivy League. If I can have a good meal on a regular basis, I'm in..." He snatches a container of Hummus and throws it in his basket. "Are you thinking of the City for school?"

I don't know how I avoided the topic all day as we talked about everything, everything except this. My body clenches up like a fist. But Noah is so distracted by all the food he doesn't notice. "Hey, look, chopped liver! I know this is totally gross, but I love chopped liver."

And now, now the lights of Zabar's and all the tiny containers of mozzarella and chopped liver are moving and spinning. I feel myself losing my breath. Shit. I put my hand in my pocket. Forget the Rescue Remedy. I want the real stuff. How do I pop a pill with him standing right here?

"Hey—"

My eyelids flip up like cheap vinyl shades.

He puts his arm around me, and it's warm like one of those floppy bean baggy things my mother uses when her neck hurts. "College is totally overrated."

Now I laugh. "Oh, yeah. That whole 'future thing.' You know 'getting a job thing' totally overrated. Would rather live in the basement of my parents' house and play video games."

After we pay for the food. He pays with a credit card, which impresses me. We walk in the early evening setting sun down Broadway. I don't pay attention to anyone walking by, because he holds the bag in one hand, and my hand in the other. I wonder if it's a buddy-type hand holding, and is this what he always does? When we were at camp, people held hands all the time on the way to meals or shops. That was the culture, I guess you could say, of camp. But we're in the New York City, not CIT land.

"Your hand is so cold," he says as we walk. "Do you want my jacket? It'll fit over yours." He stops and moves over to the side of the sidewalk. We are right in front of one of those grocery stores that reek of Asian food and rotten produce. But that smell dies away as he puts his heavy brown suede jacket over my shoulders. I feel his touch on the top of my arms. He takes his time arranging the jacket and looks in my eyes the whole time. We giggle at nothing, at the kids in puffy jackets that almost knock us over. At the woman on a cell phone carrying a bag of groceries that walks around us.

And it's at this moment where the day sort of stops. I look at Noah's imperfectly beautiful face; slightly cooked, longish nose, slightly larger bottom lip from his top, and teeth straight except one on the bottom turns in slightly. He's tousled but well groomed. He looks like Columbia or Harvard.

And as we continue to walk, and he keeps his hand in mine, rubbing his thumb over mine, which— thank God— is not raw and oozing from my biting, I wonder who I am. I never thought of myself as a girl who had fun kissing boys here and there. And I always think of myself as a good girl. A girl who would have a boyfriend...Justin... or nothing. But being in the City and being with Noah makes me forget my life right now.

We finally get to my mother's office. I open the glass door and show the security guard my ID and then loop my arm through Noah's.

We don't talk on the ride up the elevator. My stomach flutters. Noah is so much more confident, grown up than at camp. He was bookish and nerdy then. Not really talkative. But by the end of camp, I saw that losing his girlfriend, a girlfriend who helped him out of his shell, who was a cheerleader to his nerd status, losing her must have made him retreat like a turtle. That summer, I know, healed him. He had fun, and he seemed to be more at peace about Mia by the end.

I unlock the office and flick on the set of lights in the reception/waiting room. It's dark, dim even with the lights on, curtains closed.

"Mom has a small kitchen in through here," I motion to the left.

"Cool, let's get our feast set up. I am starving."

We talk about indie movies. He loved *The Waitress*. Books, he's read *The Fountainhead* that Barb just gave to me to read. We talk about everything but graduating and our futures. I'm grateful to Noah for understanding and that is the one thing that clicks in my brain about him at camp. When I didn't want to stay, when I tried to pack up and go home, he came to my bunk and let me cry my brains out. Then he calmly helped me understand how much I needed to stay, but I never felt judged.

I'm far away from everything that's stressful. I'm in a bubble where the anxiety and worry are outside and inside it's just me and this beautiful boy. Part of me worries about this. Am I addicted to beautiful boys? Before I can contemplate that, Noah leans over the spread of food, which is on the floor of the office on a chenille blanket that I know my mother has forgotten she has, Noah leans over and rubs a piece of sushi to my lips. I have just finished a mouth full of potato knish, but it occurs to me that Noah may be making a move.

I've eaten just enough to take the edge off my hunger. It would be smart to stop there if I planned on rolling around with Noah at some point.

I swallow my knish and kind of arch my body a little and lean into the sushi with my mouth open. I try a sexy smile but then all that rice gets jammed in my throat. I cough a little... and a little more... and then—

"Hey—Oh *shit!*"

I can't breathe, and Noah leaps up and grabs me so I am standing and he wraps his arms around me and starts to give me the Heimlich maneuver.

My life is defined by ironic moments. This is how my parents met, at Central Park. My mom was a young single mother to Barb, who was two-years-old. What happens was, Barb choked on a hot dog and my father, then a 32-year-old bachelor, came to the rescue and the rest is history.

Will this be my "how your father and I fell in love" story?

The piece of food comes flying out and plops right into an open container of hummus. Noah keeps his arms around me and rests his head on my shoulder.

"Jesus! It's a good thing I was a boy scout."

And I know it's sort of, maybe obscene or maybe absurd, but his hot breath near my neck and his body rubbing against me from behind and his hands so close to my boobs...it's all too much and even though I probably have some food stuck in my teeth and even though my plan was to finish chewing the sushi and excuse myself to brush my teeth in the bathroom with one of the unopened toothbrushes Mom keeps in there, even though all those things, I still want to kiss Noah. Right. Now.

I put my hands over his, which are large and smooth with a small patch of hair. I find that incredibly sexy, manly.

"I'm okay," I say, and I ever-so-barely move my body, press a little tiny bit into him.

I hear him breathe and then I breathe. My cell phone rings, not too loud. It's the alarm ring that I assigned to Sean.

"Do you want to answer that?" Noah whispers.

I really don't. I really really don't. Sean thinks I'm with Barb, having a sisterly weekend. He doesn't even know about the email from Noah. I don't even think I ever told him about Noah.

There's another moment where my phone rings again, and Noah and I freeze but now his hands are up a little higher and mine are still on his.

"No," I say. "It's fine."

It rings again.

"Are you sure?"

I worry that I'm missing the moment, a moment that I probably won't get again. He will go off to school, and I will... Maybe wind up in a nut house or rocking in my parents' basement.

But, screw it.

The phone rings again and I, Maddie Good Girl Hickman, take beautiful Noah's golden smooth hands and put them on my breasts, over my sweater, and turn my head to the side. There's a moment where I worry he might tell me something totally insane like, no or stop.

But he doesn't and I, Maddie Good Girl Hickman, cheat on my not-really-boyfriend boyfriend.

Our lips kind of crash, and it could be awkward, but I think we are equally turned on by the day and the moment. The phone makes its final plea. But I'm turned around now, and we are against one of the maroon walls. My back hits the light switch and— oops— there goes the light.

We don't say anything. Not one word.

I don't know how much time passes, but we eventually move from the wall to the love seat by the window. He pulls me close by the waist then runs his hand up—not under the shirt but over. I slide my hands around his neck and kiss him back. He rubs the top of my thighs and I stop kissing him for a minute, breathless. His mouth is on my neck while his hand slides up between my legs, again, over my clothes.

We touch like this for a while. At one point he says, "Columbia is looking better and better." To which I reply, "NYU is next door," A few minutes later he says, "We didn't hook up at camp because...?" I don't miss beat, "We were grieving widows." We laugh as we kiss. To anyone else, that would be offensive. I run my hands through his longish soft hair and sigh.

Then his cell phone rings and, at first, he ignores it but it continues. He reaches over and grabs it from the end table.

"It's my mom." He looks at me and gives me a lopsided smile. "I'm supposed to meet her back at the hotel around 8." He glances at his cell again. "It's about quarter of."

I stroke his arm and he takes my hand and kisses the palm. "If I decide on Columbia—"

"—and if I actually make it to college."

We laugh again. I tug my clothes back into place, and he runs his fingers through his golden locks. We clean up the remains of dinner and before we walk out the door, he pulls me in for another long kiss.

When he walks me back to the subway, he stops. "Let me know what happens with college and everything."

I nod, and we wrap our arms around each other without talking and then the train bumbles in. We hug until it stops in front of us.

The doors open, and a clump of people spill out.

He grabs my hand one last time and I whisper, "Bye, Noah," and step into the train.

I sit down in the first empty seat and look out the window. Noah waves to me and I wave back. No reason to tell Sean. No reason at all.

CHAPTER THIRTEEN
NERDY HOT

I sit on the couch with a worn copy of *Bird by Bird*, what I consider the premier writer's bible. A mug of chamomile tea beside me on the coffee table. What I would do for an over sugared latte right now. I couldn't fall asleep right away last night. Sean left me three messages. I finally called him back. We made plans for this morning.

Sean.

I check my cell phone for the fifth time. Just a few minutes. I run my fingers through my hair and then gather it into a ponytail with the scrunchie from my wrist. I unwrap the blanket from around my shoulders and down the tea, cold from sitting out on the counter where Mom left that and a note for me. She and Dad went into town for breakfast.

I read one more paragraph from *Bird by Bird* from the chapter called *Some instructions on writing and life*. She is supposed to be talking about how you have to "let go" of writing a perfect first draft.

I circle the passage and scrawl next to it in the margin, "Perfectionism=Walking Dead Person" and then "note to self: have more fun." I shut the book, kissing it like the Torah, and then head to the bathroom to put my make-up on. I rehearse my greeting to Sean on the way:

"What did I do this weekend?" I stop at the doorway of the bathroom thinking of a good alibi. Alibi is way too strong of a word.

I try again in front of the mirror in my bathroom. "Hey babe!" Sean and I are not on that level of pet names. *Babe.* Really? I yank my ponytail out and fluff my hair, which needs to be washed. It's lying dull and flat.

I flash a toothy grin and say in a voice way too loud: "Why didn't I answer my phone? Oh, I couldn't get a signal in the City...Yeah, Dad and I went in to the City and we had this great day..."

Oh God. My face falls. Barb, Barb and I were supposed to be together. I've never been a good liar.

This time I relax and keep my voice even, "I ran into an old camp friend in the City..."

·   ·   ·   ·   ·

"Hi," Sean says shyly when I open the side door. We smile at each other and my heart surges.

"Hi." Those big brown eyes. The guilt creeps in when he kisses me on the lips. But when I kiss him back, the guilt recedes like a tide.

I shiver from the cold air of the open door. He steps in and closes it behind him.

"How was the competition?" I say taking his coat and hanging in on a hook in the mudroom.

"I won best lead actor!" His nose crinkles with his grin. Adorable.

I hug him. "That's awesome!"

He hugs me back, lingering with his face in my neck. "But I missed you. I called you three times." The tone is not accusing, more embarrassed.

"I missed you, too. I was in the City all day. Got in late." Technically, I did miss him...and technically I was in the City...

He kisses me lightly sending little shivers down my spine. "How are we going to get through my Christmas break?"

My mouth hovers near his. I smell toothpaste and cologne. "You only live an hour away."

He sighs and pulls away a little. "My parents just booked a trip to see my sister in Colorado. Skiing at Crested Butte."

I don't have to force my disappointment. "For how long?"

"Two weeks."

"Then we better make up for any lost time now."

He grins and pulls me into his arms for a longer kiss.

When we break away, we're both breathing hard. "My parents are gone for a few hours," I tell him hoping to show him my room for the first time.

He takes both of my hands. "Actually, there's something I want to talk to you about."

My heart jumps all over the place in my chest. "Let's sit," I say, more for me than him.

We sit next to each other. He puts an arm over the back of the couch and faces me. My hands rest in my lap.

"Being away this weekend I had some time to think about...us. It's been awesome to hang out with you over these last weeks. To be honest, if it weren't for theater and you...I might be out in Colorado with my sister."

I cannot stop my brain from flashing to Noah and I joking about NYU and Columbia next year, but I push it away and focus on Sean.

"It's been fun to hang out with you, too." I squeeze his hand for good measure.

He keeps my hand in his and looks me in the eyes. "I know this might sound corny and everything...But I want us to be together, uh...officially."

Inevitably guilt, like the tide it is, returns.

"God, I sound so seventh grade. 'I like you. Do you like me? Check the box: yes, no, maybe.'"

I laugh. "*Maybe?* Maybe I like you? Man, that's worse than no. I hope you never gave a girl that option in seventh grade. Girls in middle school are bitches!"

"Tell me about it. Seventh grade was not my year. Buck teeth and braces."

"I bet you were adorable."

"No, you were adorable. I was a hopeless dork."

"Was? Was a dork?"

He makes a face and then grabs me into his arms. I pretend to fight him and say, "You said it. I'm just agreeing."

"Dork it is." He makes a geeky face and says, "Madeline Hickman will you be my girlfriend?"

Watching him make his teeth all bucked out and crossing his eyes, he's still hot not to mention sweet. A little nerdy, but nerdy hot. On paper this is the boy that qualifies the best for position of Boyfriend.

I do my own geeky face and say, "Of course, Sean. Of course, I will."

· · · · ·

My parents come back a little early, interrupting my plan to show Sean how soft my bed is.

Dad and Sean get a fire started in the family room and sit, enjoying the fruits of their labor. Sean's only been my boyfriend a few hours and he's already stepped to the first task, talking about particles and molecules with Dad. That brief stint as a physics major is paying off.

Mom and I are in the kitchen making coffee.

"I like this boy," she tells me pouring cream into Dad's mug.

"Me, too," I tell her dumping sugar into my cup.

She reaches for a spoon in the drawer behind us. "Fairfield isn't far from home and it's a good school."

I shoot her an I-don't-want-to-talk-about-this look.

"Honey, with Sean there, it would be easier."

"Mom, stop." God make the decision to go to school based on a boy? Who is this imposter calling herself my mom? Oh wait, the same person who thought it was fine for my sister to give up art school to stay close to her then boyfriend who became her husband—ex-husband. *Right*.

Mom's got concerned face on, eyebrow deeply furrowed, slight frown. I don't want my perfect afternoon with Sean ruined, so I arrange my face to reflect her expression. She bursts out laughing. "Do I really look like that?"

"Yes, Mom, you do."

She holds her hands up. "I get it. 'Butt out, Mom.'" She reaches out and strokes my face and then a strand of wayward hair. "Sorry. I forget how grown up you are getting."

I catch her hand in mine and say, "Remember how Dr. Foster said you had to let go and you know, let me figure it all out?"

She nods and squeezes my fingers. "Yes. And, sweetie, you are doing a fine job of working it out."

· · · · ·

Later, when I stand at the door again to say goodbye to Sean he says, "By the way I read that chapter you sent me."

"Yeah? "I go from normal temp to a hundred degrees in just moments. "So...?"

"It was amazing. And I'm not just saying that because I'm your boyfriend."

The word boyfriend floats in the air.

"Boyfriend," I whisper back.

"Yeah, your *boyfriend* likes your writing." He strokes my hair. "And your *boyfriend* likes your lips." He kisses me. "And your boyfriend likes your—" He squeezes my butt.

I swat at him playfully and give him a final kiss.

Boyfriend. I have a boyfriend, and it feels really good.

.   .   .   .   .

Later in the afternoon, the air still and cold, my feet slap the asphalt as I run out of our neighborhood. The sky is gray, and it smells like snow. Instinctively I make two lefts out of my street and run towards Justin's house. A million thoughts flood me as I get closer to his street. How is he doing? Does he ever come home? How come I never run into his mother anymore? My legs burn as I ascend the hill that leads to his street.

"What are you doing, Maddie?" I stop and look at my feet. "I don't need to moon over Justin anymore. I have a new boyfriend, a real one, not just one based on memory, thank you very much." I do a U-turn and head home.

CHAPTER FOURTEEN
REWRITE

Sean opens the door before I knock. "Welcome to the castle," he says and kisses me on the lips.

I step inside. Only one window, long and thin, in the whole room. "You mean prison cell. Good God don't they know lack of light causes seasonal depression disorder."

"No kidding. Why do you think my roommate is always at his girlfriend's? She actually does live in a castle. It's called the all-girl dorms."

"You could cross dress." I offer and take off my jacket.

"Are you saying I could pass for a girl?"

I hand him my jacket. He hooks it on the back of his door and closes it with his foot.

"No way." I glance around. A small bucket of cleaning supplies tucked into the opposite corner and some laundry neatly folded and stacked on his bed. Textbooks and supplies lined up neatly on his desk. "But you keep house like one. I've never seen a guy's room so pristine."

"You've seen a lot of guys' rooms?" He unzips his hoody and tosses it over my jacket.

"No." I sit down on his narrow bed and bounce a little.

"What can I say...I'll make a good husband someday."

"Or wife," I crack.

"Ohhh you are witty tonight!" He grabs me into a hug and tickles me under the arms, which turns into sliding his hands up under my shirt and kissing me long and deep.

When we come up for a breather I groan, "Ten days apart. I don't know if I can go that long."

"We can talk on the phone."

"Yeah that's nice but…"

"Maddie Hickman are you using me for my body?"

"Absolutely."

He cups my face before kissing me again. "Stay the night."

"I would," I say. "But I have those pesky things called parents and I live in their house and my mom is already on edge because Barb and I are going to Cali without her." He draws lines on my neck with his tongue making it more possible for my mind to figure out a way to have a sleepover. But I know I can't, so I rattle on, "Not to mention we both have very early flights to catch tomorrow and my sister will kill me if I'm not bright eyed and bushytailed for our trip. She hates to fly. And since Cliff can't join us—you *know* I'm so sad about that."

Sean mumbles into my neck, "Hate to miss any lectures on the Sober Life."

I take his face in mine and remind him, "We have two hours till dinner, by the way."

"What to do…what to do?" He pushes the hair out of my face.

"Well, since you love the whole house keeping thing…Maybe I can play the maid and you can play my dirty boss."

He rolls me over so I'm on top of him. "Didn't know you're into role play."

"Oh yeah. All the time. French maid. School girl." I bend over him. My hair brushes his face.

He laughs and grabs a handful of my hair, letting it trickle between his fingers. "We don't need to play pretend," he whispers. Tingles dart down my body. My hands under his shirt. Glide along the muscles of his chest.

"No pretending," I whisper back.

He kisses me long and deep. Thoughts and feelings become fluffy and sweet. Where will my fluffy and sweet come from for the next ten days?

.　　.　　.　　.　　.

The vibrations of the plane make my cup of Diet Coke (caffeine free) shake. Barbara doesn't notice. She's asleep. I sip my soda and hold a pen in my hand posed over my notebook. No words on this page yet but words on other pages. A lot of words and a lot of pages. Who knows if I will keep those words. "Mya" has made it through the Christian cult minus her star of David. She's back in her car and on her way to California. (She has pepper spray in her bag and a pocket knife so don't worry, and this isn't turning into one of those kidnap flicks on good ole Lifetime Movie Network.) I reach for the can of Diet Coke and pour a little more into the shaking plastic and press my pen to the paper.

Before we begin the descent and after the captain comes on the speaker and says a few unintelligible words that have something to do with the weather, I finally put down the pen and close the notebook. Barbara stirs and switches sides to sleep. She opens and closes her mouth. I count ten opens and closings before returning to my work to count the pages I have written in the last four hours, with only three bathroom breaks and several rounds of Diet Coke: Eighteen pages and on page seventeen begins the reunion scene of Dylan and Mya at the rehab.

My hand throbs and I wiggle the fingers and stretch back my palm. Barbara's eyes open, but she doesn't move from her sideways position, face against the back of the seat.

"Are we landing?" She asks, eyes still closed.

I clutch my pen, inspired to write a bit more. "Not yet."

She nudges me and opens one eye. "You're writing."

I look at my pages. "Rewriting."

"Story of my life, Maddie. Rewriting is the story of my life." She puts her hand on mine and closes her eye again.

I know she isn't talking about writing.

I touch my pages. Back to work.

•   •   •   •   •

Lemonade. Fresh cut grass. Lawn mower going in the distance. Air plane flies overhead. No wind. Sixty-five degrees. Warm for this time of year in San Francisco.

We sit on the screened-in porch of Bubbie's townhouse. My fingers are lightly wrapped around a clear pink glass of cold lemonade. Barb is downing Madeleine cookies. My stomach is slightly bloated from all the soda on the plane, but I manage to squeeze in some lemonade.

"Tell us about Sean." Bubbie snatches her first Madeleine from the ceramic plate.

I blush.

"Ohhhhh! Could this be love?" asks Joyce, Bubbie's best friend and partner in everything from yoga retreats to the occasional (double) *JDate*, online dating for Jewish singles.

"Is it?" Bubbie asks sipping her lemonade.

"I don't know." I hold the glass of lemonade in my lap. "Like, it's really strong like."

Joyce shakes a long finger at me, the nail is short and square. "You're young. Don't get hitched too soon. Don't do what I did, get married at twenty and bang out a bunch of kids. Then find out your husband is in the closet."

"Oh, Maddie's gaydar is pretty good now, thanks to Peter!" Barb cracks.

I reach over and nudge her arm and add, "I won't be banging out kids and getting married any time soon!"

"I almost did," Barb says.

Bubbie reaches out and strokes Barb's knee.

"Is the divorce official?"

Barb puts her third Madeleine down. "Papers have been signed and filed. Now we wait for it all to go through."

Bubbie and Joyce murmur words of support. I stay silent.

"There's not much else to say." Barb plays with a piece of cookie, pinching it and then letting it fall back on to the plate.

"We are definitely better off apart, Michael is doing something he wouldn't be doing if we were still together because he was worried about leaving me alone." Barb takes a long drink of lemonade. "I'm going to be a teacher, have my own job and money. Take care of myself. Something I would have never done if Michael and I stayed together."

"And this new fellow, he's a good man?" Bubbie wipes a crumb off the table.

"Hard to top that Michael, though!" Joyce laughs.

Barb isn't insulted by that. She just kind of chuckles and says softly, "Yeah, it is hard to top Michael. But Cliff is good man. A wonderful man."

I squeeze my eyes shut briefly to resist the roll of my eyes.

"I don't want to lecture you, Barb, but it's kind of soon, you know?" Bubbie says.

Thank God that Bubbie said it because no one else has. But not even Bubbie can get through to her because she just gushes, "He's amazing, Bubbie. He gets what I'm going through because he's been through it." Barb rattles the ice in her almost empty glass. "You know, one day at a time."

"Why couldn't you stay with Michael and still change and grow?" Bubbie asks. I've been wanting to know the answer to this one too.

Barbara looks out into the clear sky and squints. "Because we were each other's best excuses. Because when you take away my drinking and all its care-taking drama, there wasn't much between us."

I pour myself more lemonade and grab a cookie, when Barbara brightens and says, "But Maddie, she has a chance to avoid all these kinds of mistakes."

I smile even though my mouth is full of cookie.

"How are you, Maddie?" Joyce asks.

"I'm good." I swallow the cookie and smile bigger.

"All ready to go off to school, then? Still want to do some writing, like your Bub?" They all are looking at me waiting for an answer.

The smile fades. Anxiety monster slowly emerges like some wacked out Muppet and scares the crap out of me.

.   .   .   .   .

Barb kneels in front of me, Bubbie has my hand, and Joyce is fanning me. I want to tell them all to get off me because I feel hot with them hovering, but all I can say is. "Muppet."

"What'd she say?" Joyce asks.

"I think she said, 'Muppet.'" Bubbie is talking.

"She always hated the Muppets," Barb says. "Maddie, can you hear me?"

I nibble something scratchy and spit it out. Indoor porch carpet. I blow a raspberry.

"I think she's okay," Barb says and gives me a hand.

"Have you eaten anything besides cookies today?" Joyce is a retired nurse.

I nod and slowly sit up, allowing Barb to pull me to her side.

Barb strokes my hair and Bubbie sits next to me with her hand on her stomach. I know her incision is still tender.

"Oh, Bubbie, I'm sorry. You didn't try and lift me, did you?"

"Of course not. Don't be silly." Bubbie says. "Eat a cookie."

"Listen, we can talk all about this later, you guys just got here. Maybe it's just the jet lag. You always take a day or two to adjust. You should take a little nap and then we can go to dinner," Joyce suggests.

I nod and let them help me settle into the couch and tuck a blanket around me.

They each kiss my head and then go into the house to let me sleep it all off.

·　　·　　·　　·　　·

I sleep through dinner and don't wake up until the next morning. When I open my eyes, I have a vague memory of them helping me get into the house and upstairs to the room I was sharing with Barbara.

When I climb out of bed, following the scent of cinnamon and apples, I feel completely rested. I walk downstairs to Bubbie at the stove flipping pancakes with one hand and using a pair of tongs to flip sausage with the other. Barb looks up from her coffee and the paper. "Hey, feeling better?"

I nod and sit across from her but think immediately of Bubbie. "Are you allowed to cook? I mean that requires standing for a while."

Bubbie turns to me, "Are you kidding? I feel great! It's been almost a month! By the way, you look so much better today."

"Thank you...I guess?"

Bubbie slides some pancakes on to three plates and then comes to the table and hands them out.

"I only eat cinnamon apple pancakes here," I tell her.

She smiles and takes a bite. "I only make them when you are here."

We all eat in silence. I put my fork down after only a few mouthfuls.

"Bubbie," I begin. "I just want to say I'm sorry about yesterday."

She pauses mid stab at a piece of pancake. "No honey. Don't be sorry."

The look Barb and Bubbie exchange makes my face get warm.

"What?" I ask putting my fork down.

Barb stuffs more pancake in her mouth but Bubbie doesn't. She folds her hands on the table and says, "What's going on with you and college?"

"And don't faint," Barb says. "It's practically Pavlovian. Someone says, 'college,' and you drop to the floor."

Barb and Bubbie wait.

"Everything is done. I just have to send it out."

"Why are you waiting, honey?"

I look out the window at the lush green outside. So pretty in California...

"Maddie, come on, what's the deal?" Barb gulps down the rest of her glass of milk and wipes her mouth with a napkin.

"You know what, fine. You guys are right." I stand up. The only way through hell is through it. A Dante quote or something. Josephine has often reminded me the only way to conquer That Which Scares The Crap Out Of You is to attack it.

"Where are you going?"

"I have my lap top with my essay and everything. I can load it all to the common application website. All I have to do is click send. No big deal."

I expect them to say, no, sit down talk to us. But the only sounds I hear are clinking of dishes and glasses.

"Good," Bubbie says. I hear the water running behind me as I head to the living room. "Because honey, you only live once. Let's get it right."

"Right," I say feeling a knot form in my stomach. "I gotta get it right." I see my laptop on the coffee table and sigh. I feel Barb behind me. "Don't over think this, Maddie. And most of all don't blow it." She hugs me and walks back into the kitchen.

I sit on the couch and open the laptop. And yet, I kind of want to blow it.

CHAPTER FIFTEEN
1-3-4

Valentine's Day. Sean and I have been together a month and a half. Although I love our weekends in his dorm or at my house, I'm hoping that tonight we can maybe drive into the City. Maybe even go to a club and listen to live music. Lately, I've wanted to get out.

So, when Sean asks me, "Hey, wanna cook tonight?" My disappointment is hard to hide.

"Hey, I make an amazing lasagna, baby." He pulls off his sweater and walks over in just his t-shirt to where I sit on his bed with my notebook on my lap.

I let him kiss me. "I know. I've had it a few times."

He stops kissing me. "Oh shit. You're bored. I'm boring you."

Sean is so sweet that I can't let him think that. "No," I say kissing him because when we kiss it's never boring. "It's just Valentine's day and I thought maybe we could do something special."

"I did plan something special, but it sounds like my something special doesn't mean the same as your something special."

There it is. That weird pause that's been happening between us lately. But we don't talk about it. Instead, Sean lays down next to me. "Forget dinner here in the dorm. That is kind of lame." He looks at me. "We'll drive into the City and have dinner and maybe do one of those horse drawn things. It'll be nice and romantic." Sean leans over and kisses my cheek. "We'll study for a little while and then get ready."

I smile and nod. He reaches for his psych book, and we sit silently, me thumbing through the pages of my notebook and him reading.

Then I look over and see his eyes half closed... 5, 4, 3, 2—

Yep. He's out. Psychology does it every time.

I doodle 1-3-4 on the cover of my yellow notebook. The same number of pages I have handwritten in this notebook. Underneath the numbers I've written in all caps: Mya and Dylan, A Love Story. I've only let Sean read bits of it. I'm afraid of how obvious I've been. The only thing he's ever said about what he's read is, *babe you are so talented.*

I reach for my laptop and save the document I had spent the last hour working on. First fifty typed out. Another twenty to go. A full-length novel is impossible. Novella is my new goal. The entire rough draft is due Monday.

Sean makes a squeak and sigh. I call this his Dying Mouse move.

I slide out of his bed. And why does he have to snore like that?

I stand and stretch. Then stare at myself in the mirror that's nailed to the back of the door to the hallway. My skin looks the best it ever has. No zits. I've been running more lately, except when it snows. And I hit send on two more college applications.

I turn back to Sean still snoring, but a silly grin spread across his face. I shake my head and climb back in bed. Something tells me we won't be making it out tonight.

· · · · ·

A few weeks pass with Sean and me in the same routine of hanging out in his dorm on the weekends and then coffee and dinner with Peter, Jack, and Susan. The future—college, graduation, prom—are items on my "to think about list."

Nothing on that list gets checked off.

· · · · ·

No school this week. Mid-winter break. Sean has school, so Susan and I are having a girls' day. It's been awhile. On the agenda: studying for our last French test, get our nails done at the mall, and grab a greasy dinner at the food court. The evening will bring movies with Sean ...the thought of which makes my stomach tighten.

But enough of that. It's A Perfect Day. February thinks it's April, which is fine with me. Blue sky. Sun and no wind. Susan and I sit on the front porch, wrapped in blankets, and in our hands, *The Stranger* by Albert Camus.

"This Meursault dude is a total tool!" Susan tosses the slim paperback to the side. "What did Mrs. Malone say about him again?" Susan never writes a thing down in this class and has maintained an A average all year. Typical. I study my ass off and maintain a B.

"He has no conscience. No feeling." I take a squeaky highlighter to the printouts of SparkNotes and underline the word "stoicism" then say, "It's a bunch of existential weirdness. *Stoicism. Nihilism. Absurdism.*" I thump the notes with my end of my highlighter.

Susan wraps the blanket around her shoulders and pulls her sunglasses down from the top of her head. "Need to get laid-ism," she says it like a suggestion.

I consider this, chewing on the end of the highlighter. "Now that might be under *absurdism.*"

"What? You've been with Sean for months! That poor boy must have the bluest balls. I mean you won't even give him a hand job." She motions with her fist.

"Susan!" I grab her hand and shove it away. Then I say, "I always thought it would be with—" I haven't said *his* name in months...at least not out loud.

Susan raises her eyebrows and says, "Justin."

I put the notes and highlighter down on the blanket. "Yes, but I'm sick of waiting for...for what? It's not like Justin's called me. For all I know, he has a girlfriend. He's moved on."

Susan rolls to her side and adjusts the glasses on her head. "You aren't hot for Sean anymore." It's not a question the way she says it, because it really isn't a question anymore. It's a fact.

"You know when we fool around, it's still good..." Because my eyes are closed, and I can pretend that he's...

"Listen Maddie, I know all those self-help books you've read would say that's you know, *dysfunctional*, that you should break up with Sean, but I think considering all you've been through, you might be the exception to the rule." She pushes the shades back on her head and looks right at me. "Sean is kind of like your practice guy. Maybe the real guy is Justin...Maybe not. But you needed to have a real boyfriend. Not one who dies or one who goes to rehab."

Touché.

"Ride the whole thing out until you can't deal with him." She grabs my book from me. "Now, let's ditch this Meursault and go get our manipedis."

Amen.

.   .   .   .   .

Sean and I see less of each other over the next two weeks. He's got midterms and I have to do the edits on my final draft. The only thing I miss is that sweet escape of fooling around. Doing without Dying Mouse or dorm room dinners is a relief.

.   .   .   .   .

Sean and I have finished dinner with my parents. It was the send-off dinner for Barb and Cliff who are set to drive out to Massachusetts tomorrow morning. Yep. Moving in together and moving on. It's the real deal because she turned her lease over to her roommate Pam. Barb will begin her first teaching job in the summer on The Cape. In the meantime, she's helping Cliff open up his new restaurant aptly called, "Cliff's." I think "B" just got her happy ending.

I want to go to a coffee shop and write in my journal, which I haven't done in months. The last entry was in November. I need some alone time, but it's too late to do that and Sean is staring at me across the table. Dreamily.

So, I say, "Mom, we'll be back in a bit for dessert."

Sean and I bring our dishes to the sink and then dash off to my room. When we walk in, the lights are off, but my computer is still on. The screen saver is a picture of me and Sean. He's smooching me on the cheek. I look like I just ate a jelly doughnut.

I turn to him once the door is closed, and we kiss. But he pulls away and says, "Oh, shoot. I have to check my email. I'm supposed to get the night rehearsal schedule for this week."

I kiss his neck. "Let's check."

Sean walks to my computer and grabs the mouse. But nothing happens.

"Oh, shit! Is my computer frozen?"

He doesn't say anything.

"Sean?"

"What's this?"

And then, "Who's Noah?"

Oh *no*.

Oh no oh no oh no.

I leap over and grab the mouse then click close my inbox. "Oh, he's a friend from camp." And someone I technically did not cheat on you with.

"There was something in there about how great it was to see you. What's that about?" He kisses my nose. "Forget it. I trust you."

I kiss him back on the mouth taking a mental eraser to my brain, but try as I might, I can't erase the guilt. But I *didn't* cheat on Sean. I probably could even tell him what happened... "Hey Sean, remember that weekend...that you asked me to be your girlfriend..." Ugh. That wouldn't go over well. Plus, in the email, Noah tells me that Columbia's freshmen orientation is in the middle of August. Could I give him part two of the tour to NYC? I haven't replied yet.

Sean pulls me on to the bed and pulls my shirt off and kisses his way from my collarbone to the top of my bra before sliding it off. I lie on my back and stare up at the ceiling. I think about what Susan said, Sean being my "practice" boyfriend. And there are things I haven't let us practice yet. I have everything *else* down. The whole lovey-dovey couple stuff.

"Sean," I whisper to the top of his head. "Let's book a hotel room for after prom."

He stops kissing my body and looks up at me, an excited smile across his face. "Really?"

I pull his face up to mine and kiss him intensely. "Really."

In the back of my mind I calculate how many weeks until prom and the number is the same number of weeks we've been boyfriend and girlfriend.

Will we even make it?

Chapter Sixteen
"Finish Line."

We made it.

My dress sparkles. A lot.

I let Jack and Peter talk me into wearing this...Barb's old prom dress. It's cocktail length, sparkling, electric blue and has a t-back. Jack found a pair of matching shoes in the City. I look down and click my heels together.

I turn from one side to the other, inspecting my arms and the slight curve of my hips. Sexy. I never think that way about myself, but this dress fits perfectly. Which is odd since Barb is six inches shorter than me.

"You look amazing!"

I turn. Sean. He wanted to see me before we left. We found out that school policy states no one over eighteen can come to prom unless they are a student at Lincoln. Jack, Susan, Peter, and I are going as a group.

"I can't wait to see you after." He wraps his hands around my waist.

I nod, and then busy myself with brushing my hair.

"I booked a room at the Radisson."

I stop brushing and push my mouth into a smile.

He wrinkles his brow at me in the mirror. "Hey, we don't have to."

I don't want to have this conversation. I made a small deal with myself that I would get through tonight no matter what. Have a blast at the prom and then lose my virginity and then in a month, graduate. A revised to-do list.

"No, no." I look back to the mirror and turn sideways again. "I'm just feeling nervous, you know, about this dress."

Sean leaps over to me and throws his arms around my waist. "You look so hot that I'm glad you are going with two guys who are dating each other." I let him hug me. I even turn and close my eyes and kiss him. When we kiss I wonder, if Sean knows me so well, hell, if he loves me so much, why doesn't he sense that something inside of me is kind of gone, absent? Like he did all those months ago in the forest.

Sean pulls away and cups my chin with his hands. "I love you, Maddie."

I open my mouth to reply. He holds my face in his hands and waits, his eyes eager and happy. But I just can't do it.

Sean's hands drop from my face. Can't ignore *that*.

"I don't know what to say." I reach out and to touch his arm, but he backs away.

"....."

"I—wish—I—wish I...I wish that I could be—" I try.

"In love with me? In love with me like I am with you?"

"...."

He takes another step back. "Thank you."

What?

"I would have never ended this, Maddie."

"..."

"I would have stayed like this." He runs a hand over his hair. "Man, am I fucked up."

"..."

"I would have let you go through with tonight, I would have let you keep trying and trying."

"Trying?"

"Trying to love me back."

"I'm sorry." I step towards him. Lame, lame, lame. But I can't think of anything else to say.

"Sorry?" He says his face shifting from composed to pissed off. "You know what? I feel sorry for all the other guys you are going to date. I feel sorry for them because you won't ever love them. You won't ever love anyone, not even that Noah guy."

I open my mouth to protest, but he holds his hand up. "I don't want to know what the deal is with him. Spare me."

"It was nothing, Sean. I saw him that weekend you went to the competition."

"You mean the same weekend I asked you to be my girlfriend?" His eyes are black and cold. "That weekend?"

I cross my arms and look away.

"You know what? It doesn't matter. That Noah guy and that Zak kid and me, you know what we were? We were just your stand-ins until Justin shows up again. I've read your writing Maddie. Come on, the end of the book "Mya" and "Dylan" wind up *together*." He smirks. "I know you aren't over him. I never said anything." He laughs. "I believed that you were falling for me. That you were writing *fiction*."

I don't bother to protest.

"And that stuff about the cult you have in there. Lame attempt to fictionalize, by the way."

I open my mouth to tell him I killed that section any way, but I keep my trap shut. I've done enough.

"The sad part for you, Maddie is you don't even know Justin, anymore. You're in love with a fantasy, and it's never going to happen. You're going to have to finally let go of this guy at some point."

I turn away from him as the tears creep in.

"But I won't be there," he adds. "You won't be able to use me again."

The sting of reality ignites anger in me. I glare at him, wiping the tears from my eyes before they fall. "You used me as much as I used you."

"What?"

"You used me. It's not like you have this booming social life. You said it yourself, you hate Fairfield."

"Are you serious?" His face is red.

We stare each other down and far away on the other side of the house I hear the side door open and close. I hear my mom and dad laugh. Susan, Peter, and Jack have arrived complete in their similar color scheme garb, all electric blue. Mom's gotta be snapping away at the pics.

"I guess you are the social life expert, with your gay husbands and freak girlfriend." He smirks, but it's a look that's more sad than angry.

The anger fizzles. I can't be mad at Sean. I deserve all this shit he's shoveling on me. I think of Bubbie, of course, my relationship guru. I think of what she said to me about Zak and Justin. "Not everything is meant to be forever. Sometimes people come into your life to show you something or teach you something." I step towards him. "You taught me how to trust myself again. That you can fall apart and then come together."

At first, flickers of understanding, of letting go, flash across his face but then he changes his mind. "The only thing you taught me, Maddie, is to never believe a girl when she says this time it will be different."

"Sean, I'm sorry." I take another step.

But he just shakes his head and backs out of the room glaring at me.

I stand very still and listen to his footsteps speed down the hallway, the voices of my family and friends grinding to a halt. Then the door opening and slamming with a BANG.

I wait to cry, to feel that heavy sadness of a break up. But it doesn't come.

·   ·   ·   ·   ·

"Close your eyes."

I feel a soft tickle on my eyelids. I blink.

"Maddie!"

"Sorry." I close my eyes again and try to focus on breathing through the tickle torture.

"You are amazingly fine."

"Yeah, I guess I am."

"Are you relieved?"

"I feel bad saying this, but yes."

Jack stands back to admire his work. "Having sisters has finally proved to be useful."

"I keep waiting to cry or something. To feel bad." I flutter my eyes at him.

"To do the usual Maddie martyr guilt?" He bends down to brush a little more eye shadow.

I stick my tongue out at him just as Peter comes into the room. He's holding his cummerbund. He's only in his tux pants and a white t-shirt.

He stands behind us, frozen, and looks in the mirror at me.

I look too. My eyes are smoky and sexy.

"You are hot," Peter says ultra-serious.

"Should I worry?" Jack says to him in the same tone.

"Actually, yeah."

"I don't think so, boys. You see, I already exposed myself to Peter once upon a time and these guys didn't work." I stick out my breasts.

Peter's face is tomato paste and Jack is howling. "Oh, I forgot. Peter is so gay that breasts frighten him. Didn't he throw-up or something after your boob fell out?"

"No, no, that was me. He fainted, and I had to smack him to life."

"With your boobs, right?"

Peter scowls and crosses his arms. "Very funny."

"My turn! My turn!" Susan comes racing into my bedroom, her dress dragging without the height of her electric blue heels, open-toe version of mine.

Jack takes a few more minutes to blush brush and eye shadow me.

"Look at my hair!" Susan says as I stand up. Her hair is long and curly thanks to some extensions. She looks like a Barbie doll. She looks amazing. We both look in the mirror.

"And our dates are a couple."

All four of us look in the mirror and laugh.

CHAPTER SEVENTEEN
PHOTOGRAPH

"We'll go park." Jack says as he stops the car in front of the curb of the Stamford Marriot.

"How hetero of you, Jack," Susan says checking her lipstick in her small compact.

"Dropping your date off at the door is not a hetero thing." Peter makes air quotes around "hetero".

"Yes, it is, Petey, and you two," she slaps the compact shut and points a blood red fingernail at them, "are the straightest gay couple I know. You're going to prom with girls, for god's sake!"

Before Peter and Jack can lecture launch into their "we aren't interested in being the poster children for gays at prom" speech, Susan moves on to me. Holding out her fist for a bump she says, "Blow it up for making it to senior prom without being tossed into the looney bin!"

My fist stays in my lap.

"Come on Maddie, let's all blow it up." Peter holds his fist up and pops it through the front seat to us in the back.

"I will not blow it up to that." Jack throws me a sympathetic look through the rearview mirror. "By the way, I never thought you'd wind up there."

"Uh, thanks, Jack."

"But I will blow it up to you dumping that tool Sean!"

"Well, he isn't a tool...we just aren't meant to be."

"But *we* are meant to be!" Peter says.

The four of us collide fists.

"To prom!" Susan cheers.

I slide over the back seat and open the door and get out. Susan follows. Peter rolls down his window, and Susan leans in. "You guys better come back."

I lean into the open window and nudge Susan out of the way. "Yeah, I want to dance with a *guy* tonight. So, you have to come back."

"Hey, no problem. I'm practically straight anyway according to love muffin over there. By the way, that dress *is* hot, Mad." He leans out the window and kisses me on the mouth.

I blush.

Jack pops his head around and says, "Keep trying, honey, but trust me, you are still gay."

More eye rolls and then Susan takes my hand, "Listen, I'm not thrilled about making my grand entrance with a chick either, but we do love each other."

I smile and squeeze her hand. "That's true. We do love each other."

We walk up the red-carpeted stairs to the double doors. I smell carnations and roses, and once we step through the threshold, I see flowers and lace everywhere. I look up and see a staircase with a sign on the railing that says, "Through the years in Photographs". Easels stand all around the foyer with bulletin boards filled with pictures of all of the class from elementary school through high school.

"This must suck for the new kids," Susan says pulling me towards a bulletin board. A class picture of me and Peter in fourth grade. Peter's hair is mop-top and mine is in perfect braids.

Just as we stop by the check-in and flash our school IDs, Valerie, our class president, in a long flowing pink gown, bustles up and envelopes us in an awkward three-way hug.

"So happy you both are here! Just know that we all accept you both...and think it's brave to," She lowers her voice to a whisper. "Come out this way."

"Easy killer," Susan untangles herself from Valerie's small but firm grasp. Then she throws an arm around my waist and plants one on my lips. "The only lady for me is my Maddie."

"Susan!" I'm still half entangled with Valerie, who for some reason won't let go. "Listen, Valerie, Susan and I are here with—"

"Come on sweet cheeks." Susan pinches my ass and then turns back to Valerie whose eyes are saucers almost floating off her face. "Hands off, Valerie. Gotta get my dirty dance on with my lady." And with that Susan whisks us off to the dance floor.

"Susan, we are not dirty dancing." I try to pull away from her.

She laughs and finally releases me. "I just love messing with that girl. You know, I think if anyone is in the closet, it's her. Get a load of that butch hairdo and those man hands—"

"That is all so wrong on so many levels."

"Come on let's go wait for our gay husbands and look at ridiculous pictures of us with braces and crimped hair."

.   .   .   .   .

We go back to the foyer with the flowers and lace and there's another wall covered with blown up pictures of our class.

"Oh my God look at that!" Susan screeches pointing to one of the pictures.

There we are: Peter, Susan, Justin, and me with our arms around each other, flashing our braces for the camera, sitting on a catamaran. This was the eighth-grade school field trip, "bonding" before high school started. The entire class went. A camping trip on a big lake in upstate New York. Justin had weed for the first time then. Some stoner kid brought a bag of the stuff, and they smoked it behind some trees deep in the woods. I caught them, but Justin brushed it off and said he'd never do it again. Two years later, he was shipped off to military school, kicked out of Lincoln High for trying to sell pot.

Suddenly I'm aware of more people standing next to me. Tracy Jesop, Jen Smith, and Jason Richards, kids I was friends with in middle school. Kids who knew Justin.

"Hey, do you ever talk to him anymore?" Jason pops a piece of gum in his mouth. He smells like hair gel and musky cologne.

I shake my head, a lump forming in my throat.

"Bet you wish he was here." Tracy, his date, elbows me.

Jen, Tracy's close friend, puts her chin on Tracy's shoulder and looks with us at the picture. "He was so cute back then. Bet he's hot now!"

I smile and try not to cry.

"You are not going to believe this." Susan isn't looking at the pictures. She has her phone out now and is reading something from it.

"What?"

"Shamus. Shamus Andrews."

"Shamus!"

"Yes...oh, god. Shit." She rubs her wrist. I'm not the only one hanging on to the past.

"What does he want?"

"To see me...right now."

"To see you? Do you want to see him?"

She puts on her game face. But then it changes, and she whispers, "I emailed him a few days ago because I found his Bob Marley sweatshirt stuffed into this bag in my closet..." She looks at all the pictures in front of us. "Look at us. Look at how young we are."

I nod. Crying like a five-year-old at this point. "Never worry about your heart till it stops beating...

"What, honey? Are you okay?"

"No...yes...I mean, you have another chance, Susan to make it work with Shamus. You should go and find out." I reach out and touch the picture of the four of us.

"Oh, Mad." She rubs her tears away before they fall, then hugs me with one arm. "Oh, Mad. You definitely aren't over Justin, sweetie."

I shake my head and when I can talk I say, "I wish he were here."

"I know."

She wipes some tears off my face. "You need to reapply some make-up, sweetie."

"Thanks," I tell her. "Seriously, thank you for being such a good friend." I take a deep breath. "Now, as for you...go."

"Are you sure?"

"Yes. Don't worry. I'll play third wheel. It's a familiar role."

"If you're sure."

"Hey, guys!"

We turn around and there's Peter, his shirt rumpled and his bow tie crooked.

"I just dumped Jack."

"What?" Susan and I say at the same time.

"Wait. What's wrong with Maddie?" Peter points to my face. "You're crying already?"

"Yes, but I'm fine. What do you mean you just dumped Jack?"

"Oh, it's not a big deal." He sighs. "We were parking the car and his phone rang. God this is such a cliché, but long story short, there has been another guy, possibly this whole time."

"No!" Susan and I put our arms around him.

"Bastard!"

"Now he is a real tool!"

Peter untangles us from him and says, "No it's not that bad. I mean since we've been together I've considered the idea of going back to girls... Actually, it was a good excuse to end it."

"Why do we need excuses?" I ask him.

"'Cause you bitches are too nice to people." Susan kisses each of our cheeks. "Sorry everyone's heart is kind of broken and everything, but I gotta run."

"What?" Peter asks.

We fill him in. "Go for god's sake. At least one of us will be happy tonight."

"What are you guys gonna do?"

Peter turns to me, and he smiles slowly. "I'm gonna be straight Peter for a night."

"Yay!" I throw my arms around him.

"Just don't you two have sex tonight, with each other that is." Susan flashes a wicked grin and then squeezes my arm. "I'm out."

We watch her go.

"Would you ever have written this scene, Maddie?"

"No way. But then again, irony and awkward moments define my life."

We look around and see that the line for the pictures is empty.

"A picture before we go in." Peter takes my arm and loops it through his.

We stand at the velvet rope and wait for the photographer to wave us over. My hand slides out of his arm, and he laces his fingers through mine. I smile and squeeze his hand. My heart is beating fine.

PART 2
ROAD TRIP

CHAPTER ONE
LIFE HAPPENS

"It looks like you don't have any hair!" I lean on the kitchen counter to peer closer at the picture.

"That's why I grew it out." Peter yanks the yearbook toward him and clucks his tongue in disgust. "How in the hell did Susan find me remotely attractive?"

"True love, baby. That's true love." I drink my coffee and look again at Peter's buzz cut in ninth grade.

"Sleep over is officially *over*...so now, can we move on to breakfast? I'm starving!" Peter rubs his stomach.

I check my phone for the time. "Something tells me we won't be hearing from Susan."

Peter closes the yearbook. "Maybe you shouldn't have given her the hotel room that you and Sean booked. "

"Somebody had to put it to good use."

"We could have."

"Peter, we did the same thing here we would have done there. Watch movies on cable and eat junk food."

"But we could've had room service and a hot tub."

"Oh god. Is this what it's going to be like now that we are both single again?"

We laugh. The phone rings. I grab it from the counter.

"Maddie?"

"Bubbie! Hi. How are you?" I look at Peter and he smiles, mouthing, "I gotta pee." I nod.

"Maddie sweetie, do you have a minute?"

"What? Oh yeah. It was prom last night and you won't believe what happened. Sean and I broke up."

"Oh, I'm sorry to hear that...Right! Your prom! Gosh, I forgot...you can tell me all about it after I talk to your mom. She there?"

"Not yet. She's on her way back from the supermarket. What's up? Everything all right?"

Silence.

Uh, oh.

"Bubbie?" A familiar burning lump forms in my throat.

"...I need to talk to your mother." She stops, and I can hear her cry.

Oh no. Nononono. Not again not again.

"The cancer is back." The words come out of my mouth before it registers in my head.

"Maddie," Mom says.

But I can't listen. This can't be happening now. Not again.

I drop the phone into my mom's hands. When did she get home? How long was she standing next to me? Where's Peter?

I back away and bump into the couch. My mom wrinkles her face in concern and reaches out to steady me, but I shake my head and watch her put the phone to her ear and continue to watch as her faces changes shape and falls.

Not again...Not again...

. . . . .

Peter tells me, "I can stay." But I say, "No...I'll call you later." He bites his lip. I tell him, "Stop worrying," and rumple his hair. "I'll be okay. Now go. I'm good."

Once the front door is closed, I run to my room and turn on the computer.

I pull on my purple wearable blanket—Bubbie bought us each one for Hanukkah—and sit down. Pushing up the over-size sleeves, I bite my lip and then type "Colon cancer reoccurrence" in one tab. While the page loads, I glance over at the Emerson College packet I took from the college fair. My breath and the hum of the computer are the only sounds around me... I jiggle my knee up and down and glance up at the page, now fully loaded. The first two links after a few ads are "Colon cancer survival rates" and "Dealing with colon cancer." My hands pause on the keyboard and tears fill my eyes. I let them fall but don't make any sounds. I click on the link about the survival rates and scan the tiny text. I don't know what I'm looking for. A statistic, hope, how to make it go away this time?

I read about previous assumptions and the need for more aggressive treatment the first time around and how the second time the rates are worse and radiation and chemotherapy and nausea and hair loss and depression and...the text mixes with my own images of Bubbie going to chemotherapy alone or sitting the bathroom shaving her own head...

I look over again at the packet, rub my nose and then pull another tab and type in Emerson College, then click on the "online application login" and punch in my user name and password. When my account loads, I click on acceptance letter. My hand hovers over the mouse, shaking a little, while my heart thumps in my chest. I do some of those ujjayi breaths I learned in those yoga classes I took with Barb. Hand finally steady, I uncheck the box for "accept" and put the mouse over the small box for "defer". Click. I save my changes and log out.

•   •   •   •   •

"Maddie?"

The sound of Mom's voice makes me quickly click out of WebMD. My eyes burn. I rub at them and try to brush away the traces of tears.

I turn to her standing in my doorway. Her face furrows.

"Hey, Mom." I make my mouth smile. "Tonight is the premier of America's Got Talent."

She glances at the computer and looks like she's about to lecture me on sitting in front of it for too long but instead she says, "Come here," and then she wraps her arms around me. I inhale the powdery smell of her face cream.

"It starts in five minutes, Mom." I close my eyes and rest into her shoulder.

"I know sweetie." She strokes my hair. "I know."

"I hope a magician wins this season. I love magicians. That show needs a good magician."

She pulls away and tilts her head to one side, her eyes red and her cheeks blotchy, make-up slightly smeared. "Honey, we should talk about Bubbie."

I busy myself with adjusting the wearable blanket, which is now draped around my waist. As I pick up my feet to avoid tripping on the bottom, I just say it: "I'll go out there this summer and help." The rest of the plan is not necessary to tell her right now. I cross my arms waiting for her reply.

She coughs and looks past me at my unmade bed and then at the clothes on my floor. I know she wants to tell me clean it up so that she can avoid responding to my statement. But she doesn't. Finally, she looks me in the eye, "Okay. Actually, that's a good idea. But not the whole summer because you need to get back and get ready for school. And Dad and I will come out for a few weeks too and Barb. Then in the fall...well, we can deal with that then."

I know we are good because she isn't shaky or crying and she is using her list-making voice, crisp and sharp.

We smile at each other satisfied that we have plan. We Hickman girls are real planners.

Of course, as Bubbie says, life happens when you are busy making plans.

CHAPTER TWO
U TURNS

My pace slows as I climb up the hill. I push myself a little harder to maintain a steady speed. My thighs and calves burn. I see *It* emerge slowly from behind the hill. Red brick chimney, gray sloped roof, white columns on front porch. I pump my legs even more and now the entire house is visible. I don't pull a U-turn. As the hill plateaus, I slow down. The shock doesn't set in right away. A "for sale" sign. If only I had let myself run by his house earlier. The cherry blossom trees and trimmed hedges don't give me any clues about where Justin's mother is. Did she move already? Where? Is he staying at school? Sweat drips into my mouth and I wipe it with the back of my hand. I run to the dead end of Justin's street and then jog around the circle, back up, the soft breeze of late spring tickles my face, and I inhale the fragrant smell of the rose bushes on the side of his house.

I run back home filled with anxiety but also courage and hope, a buzz of energy. I deleted his number from my phone months ago, but somewhere I still have a handwritten piece of paper with his home phone number. I rummage through my desk in my room and *ta-da*!

I press the numbers with tremblely fingers.

"Hello?"

I grip the phone to my ear. "Hello, is this Mrs. Mallano?"

Pause. "Yes, yes, it is. Can I help you?"

"Hi, uh, this is Maddie. Maddie Hickman."

"Oh! Gosh, I thought it was a call about the house. How are you, dear?"

"I'm good. How are you?"

"We're selling the house. I bought a place in Florida. Gosh, you must be graduating soon, right?"

"Yes, tomorrow."

I hear her sigh. "Time certainly flies! I suppose you are looking for Justin? I assume you aren't calling about the house for sale, right?"

We both laugh. The butterflies inside fly everywhere, not just in my stomach. "No, no. I'm looking for Justin." Saying it out loud makes my body shake a little. I sit down on the stool by the counter.

"He's actually with his Uncle Tony for a week. They're fishing in Rhode Island. We're moving a few weeks after he returns, but I can have him call you or better, give you his cell phone number. I'm not sure what kind of service they have out on the boat but let me give it to you."

I write the number down on the same wrinkled piece of paper with his home phone number and thank her. Before we hang up she says, "I hope you reach him. I know he'd love to hear from you."

"I hope so, too," I tell her.

"And happy graduation, Maddie. Congratulations!"

.   .   .   .   .

I call the number from my cell before I lose my courage. It goes right to voice mail, which isn't even his voice. Just the automated woman repeating his number. I'm jealous of that woman saying his phone number. Doubt trickles in but I don't hang up. When the tone beeps, I freeze, nothing for three full seconds and then: "Hi Justin. It's Maddie. I called your house and your mom gave me your number. Uh, I just um...wanted to catch up." I shake my head. *Catch up?* "Anyway, you have my number now on your phone so call me when you can. Bye."

Now I have to wait. I lean against my bureau and count my breaths. This is harder than it sounds because my breath is running away from me, and I'm desperately trying to catch it.

I fall asleep with the phone in my hand and a few times wake up to make sure the sound is on and that it's set to vibrate. It doesn't make a peep all night. In the morning, I check the voicemail anyway. Only old messages from Peter and Susan. I lie on my back and hold the phone to my chest. "Call me back," I whisper to no one. "Just call back."

·   ·   ·   ·   ·

When the phone buzzes, my body jolts. I open my eyes. I fell back asleep. The phone buzzes again. I search for it in the covers and then, "Hello? Hello?"

"Maddie?"

"Yes," I'm out of breath but I don't want to sound deranged. I sit up and slow my breathing. I got you, breath!

"Hi, it's me. Uh, Justin."

I let the sound of his voice seep in.

"I got your message and we're on this boat..."

I hear a loud honk in the background and the sound of water splashing. "Listen I can't talk for long, but I just wanted to tell you that I'm glad you called. I sent you all these emails awhile back and when I didn't hear back from you, I thought that—"

"When?"

"November."

When I was a mental case and deleted my inbox. Right. Of course.

I hear more noise in the background. "Listen," he's practically yelling now. "I'm coming home for a week and then I'm supposed to go out to California and stay with my uncle but maybe—"

"*California?* Like the California that I'm going to?"

"You're going to California?"

"Yes! Where will you be?" Now I'm yelling and not because he's on a boat. My heart is so excited it wants to jump right out of my chest.

"He lives in San Francisco."

I break into a smile. "You won't believe this." I yell. "I'm going to Bubbie's in San Francisco."

Chapter Three
Graduation

Around me, my fellow classmates float in billowing clouds of graduation gowns. Some turn backwards in their desks, others stand up and lean against the radiator and still others sit on top of desks. Snippets of their conversations I've heard many times before drift by me like those eye floaties you get when you're tired.

"...that party was so crazy!"

"...I was sooo high..."

"...she was such a freak..."

"...I totally hooked up with him..."

To my left is Kim Ingraham, who, like me, sits properly in her chair and is not (and never has been) one to engage in post-partying banter.

She catches my eye and says, "Should we finally tell those idiots to shut the fuck up?"

"That would be the perfect way to end high school," I say and reposition my cap that, despite endless amounts of bobby pins, keeps sliding to one side of my head. "Besides, no matter what they tell each other, they are not the cool ones."

"In real life everyone knows Nerds Rule!"

We fist bump and laugh.

"Actually, I'm going to miss—" I gesture to the crew of jocks and princesses. "—this."

She smiles, and I see the tiniest drops of water in her eyes. "Me, too!"

"Okay, ladies and gentlemen, it's show time." Mrs. Marino yells over all the noise.

Kim and I leap up at the same time then giggle nervously. I take a few breaths and mutter to myself, "Okay, time to push your stomach down and get in line, Hickman."

"What?" Kim leans into me. "You're not gonna throw-up, are you?"

"No!" I nudge my cap back to center again. "Not yet, at least."

.   .   .   .   .

My high heels click on the pavement as I follow behind Johnny Holden. Our gowns blow behind us like sails on a sailboat. Patchouli tickles my nose and a fainter smell, which despite my lack of experience, I identify as pot, wafts by. For the first time ever, my class doesn't talk much. Just the tapping of our footsteps, and the wind rustling our gowns. Up above, not a cloud in the sky or a drop of humidity in the air. As we approach the tent on the lawn outside, the school band plays *Windy*. Teachers and parents turn around to watch us march to our seats. The administration, gray haired men and women in dark suits, line up on the stage, smiling.

I crane my neck, but don't see my family. No Susan. No Peter. Nobody. My cap keeps melting off my head like ice cream. I push it back into place. It slips again. I find my seat and with one hand on the cap, lower myself carefully onto the metal folding chair.

"Madeline!" Holding my cap for dear life, I turn around to see who's calling my name.

"Bubbie!" A knot of tears bunches up in my throat.

"We're over there," she says pointing to the far, left corner of the tent. My dad holds his video camera, Barb has the regular camera around her neck and Cliff, looking uncomfortable in khakis and a tie, his braids blowing in the wind, is showing her how to use it, and Mom—no kidding—is holding a box of Kleenex. They all wave simultaneously like at a football game. I wave back and hiccup. The knot of tears is choking me.

I watch Bubbie go back to her seat, her floral dress billowing behind her just like my graduation gown. Gasping like a guppy, I rub my eyes, sure that the mascara is already running down my neck.

Someone knocks my hat completely off my head.

"What the—" I catch it before it slides to the ground. "Damn thing. Bane of my existence!"

Susan grins at me, not noticing my capless head, then she growls at Johnny Holden. "Move out, John-boy!" She tells him he has to switch seats with her, and Johnny is so high that he gets up and leaves. To where, I have no idea. Maybe to smoke another doobie. "Hey, John, where can I get some..." I stop. Somehow graduation isn't the right setting to make my first weed purchase.

Maybe Bub and I will smoke together when I go out to California. Helps with the side effects of chemo. I once asked one of my shrinks if I automatically should avoid drugs and alcohol because of the family history. They claim I don't have to worry but should keep an eye out for signs of trouble like drinking or smoking daily. But I can't even take Rescue Remedy without worrying.

But I don't have to worry about it today, because I LEFT IT AT HOME. I tell this to Susan and then add, "I should have stuck it in my bra."

Susan wrinkles her brow and pulls at the top of my gown. Peering down, she says, "Na, not much room in there, chickie. By the way, you might want to substitute that white cotton for lacey underwire." She winks at me.

I push her hand away. "It's graduation, Susan. Not a date."

We look at each other and then together let the full impact of the word hit us. "Whoa! Graduation!" We high five.

"Now help me re-pin this stupid thing," I order her.

She places the cap on my head and expertly pins it into place. I touch it. It doesn't budge.

"Hey, don't you have to be up there?" I ask her.

"Not yet. Look around. This is gonna take a while," she says.

"You're not nervous?"

"Nope."

The band plays a rousing rendition of *U Can't Touch This*. We shake our heads. Another stupid thing I will miss...our awesome band playing outdated tunes.

"I have some news."

"You're coming to California with us?"

"Noooo."

I pout but then say, "Spill it."

She tries to suppress a smile, but I can see the corners of her mouth quivering, "This morning Shamus asked me to go to the Cape with him!"

"For the whole summer?"

She nods. "I'm helping him and his brother with the opening of their tattoo shop. Lounge around the beach, relax...Maybe go eat at Cliff's place with B." We both roll our eyes.

"And your parents are totally fine with it, of course."

She beams. "I vow to never complain about their clueless asses again."

U Can't Touch This ends. No one claps.

"I'm going to miss you!" We squeal like little girls.

"We'll see each other, Maddie. You're planning on visiting your sister." She grabs my hand. "We have to pinky swear."

"We've never in our lives uttered those words..."

"Pinky swear!" She demands.

I hold my pinky to hers. "Pinky swear!"

We listen to more bad music—*Don't Stop Believin'*— and watch Johnny Holden look for his seat and promptly trip over nothing.

"Where's Peter?" I ask.

"He won't leave his seat. He's worried the dean is gonna find him in someone else's seat and renege his diploma!"

I laugh. We watch the rest of the alphabet file in.

"I can't believe Daddy Homophobe said yes to the California deal. Does he know that Peter's new boy-toy is driving?" Susan asks still watching the line creep by us.

"I wouldn't call Larry a boy-toy. Peter claims they're only friends. He's still recovering from Jack. So, Peter's new friend," I put air quotes around friend, "is driving us all in his red convertible."

"Wind in your hair..." Susan says.

The line of white robed classmates has stalled. The wind blows white silky polyester all around us, in our faces. We laugh, trying to escape the onslaught.

Susan tucks a lose strand of blonde hair into her cap. "Ready to tell your parents the slight changes in your plan?"

"Not at all." I play with the blue and white tassel that dangles from my cap. "I'll tell everyone later. It's not a priority right now." I drop my hand onto my lap, smoothing the creaseless fabric.

Then we hear, "Hey!" and turn to see Peter. The gown swishes in the breeze around him. He puts his hand on the front of the gown, and it falls flat for a moment.

Susan and I wave.

"Can't believe you made it over here!" I say.

We all hug and kiss. Then Susan says, "I gotta go be with the gray hairs." She straightens her hat and pulls out a tube of lipstick from nowhere and slides it on. "I might be the hottest valedictorian this school has ever seen!"

"And the most modest," Peter gibes.

We watch her run up the aisle towards the stage, her gown flowing like a super hero cape around her.

Peter puts his arm around me. "How are you holding up?"

"Fine."

"Liar." He squeezes my shoulder.

"Just want to get this over with," I say.

"So we can get to the road trip."

"Yes!"

"So you can get to old Blue Eyes," he teases.

"And Bubbie," I add.

"Bubbie is right over there," he says.

"Smart ass."

Then the band stops, and everyone hushes a little. We sit down.

"This is it!" Peter whispers. "Look at her up there! She looks beautiful."

"I know." I watch Susan stand up at the podium adjust the microphone and a delicious chill of happiness fills me. Susan, Peter, and I. Still together.

"Shamus asked her to go to the Cape. They'll be minutes from Barb and Cliff. We can make one trip and see them all."

"Really? He better not break her heart."

"Better to have lost at love—" I begin.

"Then never to have let yourself love an asshole," Peter snickers.

"That doesn't even make sense, Peter."

"Whatever...Love sucks."

I sigh.

"Except for you and Justin, Maddie. I think it's the real deal."

I can't find a reply for that one. Peter gives me one last hug and runs back to his seat.

"Welcome to the last day of childhood," Susan begins her speech.

That's right, if childhood ends in a few hours, then adulthood begins, and as an adult, I decide my future—not my parents.

Now, I'm ready to graduate.

CHAPTER FOUR
"DON'T YOU THINK YOU SHOULD HAVE TALKED TO US FIRST?"

It's midnight when I walk into the house. Bubbie is on her way home. She had to get back immediately for her treatment on Monday morning.

The smart light flicks on as soon as I close my car door, and it splashes onto the driveway as I walk to the side entrance of the house. I take my shoes off before I cross the threshold into the mudroom. I do not want to wake whichever sleeping parent is resting in the living room. As I tip toe into the kitchen and head towards my room, I hear a rustle and then, "Maddie?"

Dad. In his favorite chair.

"Hi, Dad."

"Hey, honey," He rubs his eyes and yawns. "Did you have fun?"

"Yeah," I whisper. He cups his hand around his ear. I repeat myself and he smiles.

"I'm really tired," I say walking towards him as he stands up.

"Listen, before you go to bed, I just want to ask you something."

I freeze.

"The admissions office at Emerson called yesterday."

My eyelids hurt from how wide eyed I am.

"I wanted to wait to bring this up to you, but they wanted to confirm that you did, in fact, mean to modify your acceptance status?"

No blinking or movement of any kind.

My dad's eyebrows furrow. He folds his arms over his maroon robe.

"Maddie, do you need to tell us something?"

"I was hoping—" to avoid this conversation totally until I was safely in California.

"Don't you think you should have talked to us, maybe, before you checked the box?" He doesn't say it like he's mad.

Fatigue rolls me over. Sweat beads up on my forehead and my eyelids fall. I sink onto the arm of Dad's chair.

My father's hand, warm and sweaty, on my forehead. "Look, go to bed. Your mother doesn't know about this because I was hoping you would tell me this is all a mistake." I open my eyes but have nothing to say.

"And apparently that's not the case. Let's sleep on this all and talk in the morning."

So, he's not going to freak on me.

He kisses the top of my head. "Goodnight, Maddie."

I watch him walk up the stairs and thank God I'm so tired, otherwise I would have a full-blown panic attack.

.   .   .   .   .

The next morning, thanks to the best night's sleep in months—I guess honesty is the best policy— over hazelnut coffee and fresh cranberry bread, I tell my parents the details about my slight change in plans for the fall. My father runs a hand over his head a million times, and Mom's face falls into a heap.

"...I'm not going to start until January." I brush the crumbs of cranberry bread off my lips with a paper napkin.

Mom hasn't taken a bite of bread yet.

"We had those sessions with Dr. Foster about all this and you were on board with starting in the fall." Dad has stopped eating too at this point, which is unthinkable.

"That was before Bubbie got sick again." I wait for their reaction. Maybe this time they'll get it.

"I don't understand." Now she puts the bread down. "She has, who knows how many months of chemo to complete." She looks at my father but continues to talk to me. "I planned to go down every few weeks. She has Joyce."

"I need to be with Bubbie. I want to be there every day. When she is sick or tired. When she needs help." I take breath. "I will stay and take care of Bubbie and go to school in January."

"I don't like this idea," Mom says.

Dad sips his coffee instead of gulps. "I don't know if the deferment is a good idea or not," he says. "But staying in California for that long? I think it's sweet to want to stay and care of Bubbie, but what else will you be doing?" He looks at my mom.

Then Mom explodes. "Stan, she is not deferring." Finally, she looks at me. "You are not deferring. I'm calling Emerson tomorrow to straighten this out."

This is so ridiculous. When are they going to get it? I stand up. "You know what? This is crazy. I've been losing sleep and getting all panicky again over this for the past few weeks and for what? For what reason? Fear of disappointing you? And now here I am full blown disappointing you both and I did not fall apart or die. I am still here. And so are you guys." I think of Susan's opening lines to her speech. *Welcome to the last day of childhood.* "I'm an adult now, Mom. You guys have to let me make my decisions, without trying to guilt me into doing what you want." And with that, I walk my adult self out of the living room, and they don't follow.

·   ·   ·   ·   ·

The rest of the week is terrible. We don't talk about anything. They don't help me pack for California. Mom doesn't volunteer to iron and fold my underwear, t-shirts, or jeans to keep them from wrinkling in the suitcase. Dad doesn't help me get my luggage out of the attic. They stand in the kitchen when I talk to Bubbie about my plan to stay and even when she asks to talk to them to make sure it's okay, they shake their heads and say, "You're an adult." It's terrible.

And that's exactly what made me pick up my cell phone and scroll through to Justin's name. A little girl sits and pines away for the boy she wants. An adult woman calls him. Faces the reality of whoever he is today.

"Maddie?"

"Justin?"

Awkward pause, but I forge ahead because I want this...whatever happens. "So, I just wanted to...um..." God what do I want to say? "I guess I want to just say 'hi'." Smooth.

He laughs. "Hi." Pause. "I'm glad you called. It was hard to talk last time."

Another awkward pause.

Pause. "How's your grandmother?" I had told him the whole story briefly at the end of our last conversation.

"She's managing...Doing chemo now. She came for graduation."

"That's good, uh, that she's okay."

"Yeah," God this is a lot harder than I thought. "Where are you now?"

"I'm in California. A little jet lagged, actually."

We laugh. Less awkward now.

"Yeah..." I've never heard Justin awkward and now I'm hearing a little hint of nervous. "I wanted to tell you that I had this whole plan, you know to try to see you again. That's why I emailed you back in November. But when you didn't answer and then Mom decided to sell the house, and I don't know, I think I also chickened out because it's like, how can I just show up at your house when we haven't talked since last year." He stops.

I want to say, you mean when we kissed in my car and it was amazing? And you said I still love you but I'm still an ass and I can't be with anyone and I confessed that I couldn't be with anyone either...because I still thought of you and then I never heard from you again.

My heart beats fast. I can't find my voice. I don't say any of that because the past is over, and I don't want to cling to it right now. Instead, I say what I want to: "It's going to be so good to see you again."

"So good," he says.

Silence but it's not awkward. At all.

"I guess I'll see you...soon."

"Yeah, bye Maddie."

"Bye, Justin."

· · · · ·

The morning before I'm due to leave, I wake up early, so early that I don't hear the sounds of coffee grinding or Mom padding around in her walking shoes before heading out for her morning power walk.

I put my sneakers on for a run because I won't be able to run probably for the week. The kitchen is dark, and the sun is rising outside. I can see the stripes of pink through the window above the sink while I drink water and eat a cereal bar.

I leave out the side door and just trot down the driveway. The air smells sweet and damp. I pass my mother's plantings in the center of our circular driveway and when I turn out of the house and pass it, I look back and view the work my mom has done on it over the years. The gardens, the re-staining of the shingles. The stone wall. We may not be the biggest house on the block, but it is the prettiest.

I run enough to return home drenched in sweat and as soon as I enter the mudroom I peel off my shorts and tank top and walk in my underwear to my room. I check my watch. 7:30. Mom should be up and getting ready for her walk and Dad might even be contemplating a run...He's back to watching his carbs this week. I stretch quickly and then shower. When I come out, Mom is in my room, suitcase opened and refolding some of my shirts.

She looks up at me and tears up. I walk to her and put my arms around her shoulders. We just hug while she cries.

"I'm sorry," she says.

I reach for the box of tissues on my nightstand. "Thanks."

She pulls a tissue out and blows her nose. I reach around and tuck the shirt back into the suitcase and rezip it and then sit on the bed. "Mom, you have to trust me."

She nods and balls the tissue up.

"I know what I'm doing." Even though I still have doubts, they don't need to know.

She nods again and opens her mouth but can't stop crying. I hug her again and tears creep in, a few fall when I close my eyes and say, "I love you, Mom. And I'll call you at every stop."

"My baby." She moves away and wipes her eyes and then mine. "Now, let's get you some coffee and snacks for the ride."

• • • • •

My father waves to Peter and Larry as they pull into the driveway. Larry pops out quickly and strides over to my father. They shake hands and introduce themselves.

"Do you have a clean driving record?" My mother furrows her brow.

"Yes ma'am. Not even a speeding ticket." She nods but crosses her arms.

"Let's load your luggage into the car." My dad grabs my enormous duffle bag.

We all busy ourselves with rearranging the bags in the trunk.

Larry slams the trunk shut and turns to my parents. "We will take good care of Maddie."

I sigh and remind everyone. "Maddie doesn't need taking care of." I hug Dad and then Mom, who hands me my favorite pillow. I take it and whisper thank you. "Seriously, I'm fine. I have my Rescue Remedy right here." I hold it up. This makes them both laugh.

After I slide into the backseat, I lean out the open top of the car, "Love you guys."

They wave and that's when I have to turn away and tell Larry to go because I don't want them to see me cry.

CHAPTER FIVE
HIT ME BABY ONE MORE TIME!

In the backseat of Larry's car wind blows my hair all over the place while "Lady B's", as the boys refer to Britney Spears, electronically enhanced voice echoes out of the topless car.

"I love this song!" Larry fist pumps the open air with one hand, holding the wheel with the other.

Peter holds an invisible microphone to his mouth and sings, *"Keep on dancin' till the world ends..."*

Then together they duet, *"Whoooaaaaooooaaa...."*

Larry switches hands and beats up the beat again chanting, "Lady B is in the house!"

My hair wraps around my mouth and nose, hiding the tears and the scowl that's growing bigger and bigger by the beat. I hug my pillow to my chest. Day 2 of Road Trip from Hell Featuring Britney Spears' Greatest Hits.

"What is this one? Oh, God. It's Hit Me Baby One More Time. Why do I know the name of this song?" I groan.

"I shouldn't have let you go! Show me how you want it to be... tell me baby 'cause I need to know! My loneliness is killing me... and I must confess I still believe..." Larry sings at the top of his disturbingly deep voice.

"Still believe!" Peter in falsetto.

"Ouch, Peter!" I cover my ears.

Peter struts as best he can in the front seat.

"When I'm not with you I lose my mind..."

"Open your eyes, Larry! You're driving for god's sake!"

"Give me a sign!" Peter grabs the wheel and grins back at me.

"Great," I mutter. "We've escaped death by smashup but not Britney."

"Hit me baby one more time!" Larry pops his eyes wide at me.

My hair sticks to my salty wet cheeks. Up above me, in the open air, the summer morning sky cloudless, dry, and not too cold. Pop music and falsetto boy voices block out thoughts that keep trying to invade my mind. Bubbie. Sickness. Hospitals. Justin...the buildup of wanting to be with him and now it's about to happen. We pass the "Welcome to Des Moines, Iowa" sign. Around us, flatness abounds, endless in all directions. But the new geography doesn't sustain me, and my thoughts wander back to confusion. Bubbie. Death. Sadness. Justin. Life. Kissing. Happiness. Confusing. Smashing into the guardrail. Zak. Justin. What if Justin's car wrapped around a telephone poll? Bubbie, bald, frail from chemo. Gone. Poof. Life over. No second chance.

My stomach rumbles. I peek my head between the two front seats and say, "I gotta eat something."

· · · · ·

We stop at a gas station that has a sign on the door that says in red KRISPY KREME DOUGHNUTS. Larry shuts off the car and gets his wallet out. "I'm going to get some gas. You guys go get some food," he says.

Peter and I go crazy and buy half a dozen Krispy Kreme doughnuts—no jelly—a liter of Diet Dr. Pepper, and a bag of pretzels. The guys already ate all of the food Mom had packed us, not even leaving me a crumb of a scone.

Peter brings the food to the car, and I go to the bathroom. I come out of the single toilet restroom, the air smells of gasoline and the sun is bright. I go back to the car and see that the roof is now on. I drink from the liter of Dr. Pepper. Peter watches me and then says, "You look like shit. Come sit and in the front and listen to bad music with me."

"No, Maddie and I need to bond. I'll keep driving with Maddie in the front. You can tackle the *Lord of The Rings* trilogy in the back seat." Larry rolls his eyes. "And do it now 'cause I don't want you reading that shit in California. We have to look cool on the beach together and that shit will ruin my rep."

"What rep? No one knows you?"

"But they will."

·   ·   ·   ·   ·

Larry opens with, "My brother died when I was only eleven. He had leukemia."

And I respond with:

"Wow." Is all I come up with because I think all the hours in the car have gone to my brain.

"He was a totally healthy kid until he was seven and I was five. I watched him slowly die for six years. At the very end, I said to him, 'I'll take care of your model airplanes.' He was obsessed with model airplanes. He couldn't talk so he just gave me a thumbs-up sign."

I put a hand to my mouth because cry-baby Maddie is about to blow again.

Larry just sits and stares straight ahead. He doesn't cry but hands me some napkins that had been tucked into the pocket on the door. I hold it to my nose, as that's the leakiest orifice on my face.

Then Larry puts his hand on my leg and squeezes it. "I'm sorry."

I glance back at Peter, but he's got his ear buds in and is reading *Lord of The Rings*.

Larry and I are silent for a few minutes and I say, "My grandmother has colon cancer." When he doesn't say anything, I continue. "That's why I want to stay out there with her. You know, to help out."

"Yeah, Peter told me the whole deal." He clucks his tongue and shakes his head. "But listen, don't paint this romantic vision in your head of you putting a cold washcloth on her head or you fixing her meals in bed. You pushing her in a wheelchair in the park. You think you will feel good about helping her and you will feel useful. But you won't. You will feel horrible. Just know what you are getting into."

"She's not in a wheelchair nor is she dying. She's got a good chance of making it, that's what the doctors say." I twist my hair into a bun and wrap my scrunchie around it.

"Yeah, they all say that. But the good ones, they'll tell you the truth."

Before I can even find a good response, he launches into:

"What's with this Justin guy?"

"Larry, I appreciate what you are trying to do, aggressively therapize me, but contrary to whatever kind of crazy Peter told you I was, I'm actually pretty good, so if we could stick to a more give and take type of conversation, that would be awesome."

"Yeah, absolutely." He looks at me sideways and gives me a thumbs-up.

Now we seem to have nothing to say. Might as well shoot an arrow in the dark, as Bubbie says. "Are you excited about the summer?"

"Yeah, opportunity to really let my gay out."

"You can't do that at home?"

"Hell no!"

"Why?"

"Parents are so-called Christians."

I digest that and then ask, "How are you even doing this whole thing?"

"My parents are rich so-called Christians, and therefore, give me things to keep me out of their way. Money, credit cards, a car. They think I'm just taking a road trip and visiting friends. They have no idea that I'm driving out here to finally see the Mecca for gays...or that I'm one of them. They don't care what I do as long as I don't get arrested or wind up in the hospital...Or come out of the closet to them. Being a criminal and being gay are the same thing to them." He adjusts the rearview mirror. "Anyway, oh look at sleepy head back there. Passed out from the boring world of midgets and elves."

I look back and Peter's head is tucked into his chest and his book open on his lap. "Peter's a light weight traveler. Car rides of just a half hour knock him out. Surprised he lasted this long."

"Got to add that to my need-to-know list about Peter."

"You have a need-to-know list?"

"Sure...any prospective fellow, friend or lover, of mine needs a full interrogation/ investigation before anything can happen."

Peter mentioned that Larry was "quirky" and since we haven't all hung out that much together, I guess I'm getting my schooling now. I call Larry quirky and slightly paranoid with a dose of who-gives-a-shit-I'm-doing-what-I want.

What should be on my need-to-know list about Justin?

CHAPTER SIX
"WE TOOK A WRONG TURN."

I open my eyes. For a few minutes, I look out the window of the backseat at the trees whizzing by. Maybe it's just my arrogant East Coast attitude, but does the Midwest really all look the same? I sit up and crack my neck, yawn and stretch, and then just sit dumbly. I look at the car clock. It is 7 a.m.

Through the rearview window Peter sees me. He has worried-Peter look. "We took a wrong turn."

I rub my eyes and mumble, "Uh, huh."

"A really, *really* wrong turn."

Bantery Larry is quiet, so I stop rubbing and try to focus on Peter's face in the rearview mirror.

"We're in Kansas," he announces.

When I don't reply, he cracks, "There's no place like home, Dorothy."

To which Larry responds, "Golly, Aunty Em. I didn't even click my heels together."

They look at me like, "Tag! You're it." But all I can say, is:

"I'm starving."

Peter glances at Larry. "Looks like Dorothy needs a refuel."

"And we gotta make it to Emerald City!"

"Enough!" I bark. "Feed Dorothy...NOW! And actually, we don't need to make it to the Emerald City because we shouldn't be in effing Kansas!"

Larry turns back and holds up his *California Road Trip Handbook* with his finger in between the pages. "We are actually just two hours off route." When I don't show any change of expression he adds, "And there's a diner coming up soon."

When we finally get to The Egg Shack, I've forgiven the boys of their driving blunder since they've agreed to pay for my meals the rest of the way. The Shack is an actual shack, with—no kidding—about fifteen trucks parked around it. It's almost 9 a.m. My stomach has been moaning so loud that Larry asked if I had shit my pants or something. I'm too hungry and still a little zoned out to banter and just grunt at him.

As soon as the waitress comes to our table, I tell her "Scrambled eggs and a side of dry toast. A cup of coffee, lots of cream and sugar."

The waitress smiles nervously, "Don't you want a menu?" She speaks with a kind of funny twang, not quite southern and wears her hair in braids. We are definitely in Kansas.

"No," I growl. "Just want to eat."

"Please excuse our rude friend. She has her period."

I throw a bunch of sugar packets at him that I was sucking down because my hunger pains hurt that bad.

The waitress laughs, but her eyes are a little scared-bunny. Maybe people don't openly say the word "period" in Kansas? I once knew a girl from camp who came from Kansas, and she said everyone is a born again evangelical Christian. Those people don't even have dirty filthy things like periods, I bet. They piss holy water as my friend told me.

Peter shakes his head. "I'll take some waffles and sausage."

Larry looks at both of us and then sighs. "Guess we won't look at the menu. I'll take an egg white omelet. You do *do* that here, right?" The waitress nods, her face morphing from scared to annoyed. By now I think she's noticed our New England/New York accents, I'm sure.

"I'll take that, and do you have some kind of latte or cappuccino?"

She nods again, her mouth now tight, and her eyes flashing.

"Fantastic! I'll take one of those."

"Which one?" She asks him and for a moment she grips that menu like she is going to strike him over the head with it.

I close my eyes and lean into Larry while we wait for our food. Even with not showering since we left (we do these quick spritzes at each rest stop, and I even have learned how to take a partial shower in the sink), he smells good, and unless it's the poor lighting, he has the face of a young blondish Tom Cruise...which makes sense since Peter is a little obsessed with Tom, and it sort of rubbed off on me.

I think I'm delirious from hunger and driving because I say, "You're kind of cute."

Larry turns his face, and we are nose-to-nose in the booth. "Thanks." He smiles, flashing perfect teeth.

But the food arrives, and no cute boy is more important than those eggs at the moment. The plate doesn't hit the table before I dig in.

Midway into the meal, while I'm done already and slumped into the corner of the booth, Peter leaves for the bathroom.

Larry asks, "You don't drink, Maddie?" He sips his cappuccino then puts it down. "Ever?"

I open one eye and maybe because I've been refueled. I shoot back, "You don't try girls? Ever?"

"Ha, ha." He waves his fork at me.

I close my eyes again and begin a fantasy of seeing Justin for the first time. His eyes...

"I'll answer you, if you tell me first."

With my eyes still closed I say, "What's with the q and a about me? Don't you want dirt on Peter, so you can fill in that need-to-know sheet of yours?

"Peter's an open book."

This time I laugh. "Hell-to-the-no! I had no idea he was gay until last year."

Larry makes a kind of noise and says, "I know the whole story."

My eyes are totally open now. "Really?"

"Really." He smirks. "No secrets. I know it all. Except I can't figure you out, and since you are the other half of Peter, now I have a need-to-know list about you."

"He's got a point, Maddie."

"You're back from your—what was that a whole shower in the sink?" I see that his hair is a little damp. "Man, you were gone a long time."

He pulls his wallet out. "I'll go pay for this while you two try to unlock the mystery that is Maddie." He leans down and kisses the top of my head, and I scowl.

After Peter walks to the register, Larry and I turn back to each other.

"I've never been drunk." I confess. "Is it a conscious choice not to drink? I don't know. It's never seemed, I don't know, necessary."

I can't tell what he's thinking by the expression he has.

"I've tried girls and...there's a part of me that thinks I'm bi."

"Bi-curious or bi-confused?" I say, very authoritative on the subject thanks to multiple trips to the Bisexual-Gay-Straight Alliance with Peter.

Larry doesn't say anything, but there's a flicker of uncertainty.

We don't continue because Peter returns and announces: "We are taking a break. A real one. With a real shower that's not in a friggin' sink. Let's get back on track to Nebraska and then we are stopping at the first decent hotel."

·　·　·　·　·

"Was your almost kiss and boob-touch with Maddie like some kind of gay test?"

Larry's been quiet for a record twenty minutes, and this is what he comes out with. I shake my head. Peter navigates the car to the left as we approach the exit for the hotel. Then he replies, "Not entirely. Although I guess you could look at it that way...And I failed that test."

I stretch my arms out and say, "For me it was a way to see if those rumors about us were true. Let's see if Susan's jealousy is founded on anything real. You know when they were a couple, she was super jealous of my friendship with Peter and when Justin and I broke up, her jealousy was nuts. I think I gave Peter my boob to see if I could stop being so friggin' depressed for five seconds." I turn back to Larry in the backseat. "Not a test for me."

Peter turns into the parking lot of the hotel.

"Sounds like you wanted Peter's shit." Larry leans forward and puts his chin on my chair.

I resist backhanding that chin and say, "I did not want his shit. But you have to admit, our whole relationship, up until that point, was kind of suspicious."

"You mean like why hadn't we ever hooked up?" Peter glances at me.

"Yeah, I, apparently, was pretty clueless about your preference for boys."

"So was I," Peter sighs.

Larry is eerily quiet.

We park the car and busy ourselves with getting our things. We rummage through our bags and throw a change of clothes and some toiletries together, all into a few empty grocery bags we find in the trunk. As we schlep to the automatic doors of the hotel, Larry says, only loud enough for me to hear, "Would you be my gay test?" Out of the corner of my eye, I see Peter. Apparently, he heard because his jaw is to the floor.

I don't answer.

.   .   .   .   .

Larry gets us a room with two twin beds and a pull-out couch. As we pass through the lobby to the elevator, we see a pool in the courtyard, glistening and empty. The temperature is about eighty degrees according to the way-too-cheery, corn fed concierge.

"Pool first. Then dinner in that restaurant downstairs," I say as Larry slides the automatic key into the slot of the door.

We push into the room, and I drop my suitcase next to the pull-out couch.

Peter goes to check out the bathroom, and Larry opens the curtains to see what sort of view we have. Parking lot...with some pink and yellow gardens. Not too bad. Then he turns to the snack bar next to the flat screen TV.

"Don't even open that, because we'll have to pay."

"You won't have to pay, Peter. I'll have to pay, Daddy will have to pay, and we are on vacation, so I say...snack bar away." He breaks the plastic strip that holds the fridge closed. As I head to the bathroom, behind me I hear bottles clinking and the rustle of packages opening.

I hear them laughing and the sound of someone sitting down on the bed. When I come out of the bathroom, Peter and Larry are sitting on the bed...drinking from the tiny bottles of alcohol. I recognize the clear liquid as vodka and then see another, more opaque bottle in Peter's hand, mint Schnapps. Barb used to frequent both poisons.

But because I'm on a road trip and because Peter's doing it, which somehow makes it seem safe, I walk over to the fridge and take inventory. Four more small bottles...two vodkas, two small mini bottles of some kind of white wine. This is supposed to be a big moment, like losing my virginity or something. Which, in a way, I am. I grab the vodka. Somewhere in the files of my mind about Barb's years drinking, I remember her telling me that vodka doesn't make you sick.

As I crack open the bottle, Larry says, "Wait! Wait! Come here." He pats the space next to him on the bed. Peter is oddly quiet and looks glassy-eyed already. I know Peter's experience with alcohol is limited to his summers in Europe, so he's as much of a lightweight as me.

We clink bottles.

"Cheers!"

"To our road trip!"

"To Maddie being reunited with Justin!"

"To helping the gays!"

"To my Bubbie getting better!"

"To—"

"To us!"

"To us!"

"To us!"

Clink, clink, clink.

Drink...drink...drink...

· · · · ·

Although we are strewn over the bed and clearly drunk off our asses, we've decided to swim.

"Pool party, bitches!" Larry says rolling off the bed and walking crookedly to his bag. Peter rolls over and lays his head on my shoulder as we watch Larry try and fail several times to open his bag. We all giggle.

"I'm gonna go, too," I say into Peter's hair. He murmurs and rolls away from me. I sit up slowly, like I took too many of the pills Dr. Foster prescribed.

I grab the bag with my stuff and rummage for my bathing suit, I whip off my shirt and pants. Shimmy out of my underwear and bra and put on my suit. The two of them stare at me with their mouths hanging open.

"What?" I say to them. Peter shakes his head. I turn to Larry and say, "Here's your gay test..." Then I shimmy my boobs. Something I'm positive I've never done in my life unless it was in a dance class or something.

Larry's eyes get big.

Peter grabs Larry's hand and pulls him towards me. "Go ahead. That's how I found out."

But I've shimmied myself too hard and have fallen backwards. This makes us crack up, and soon we forget my boobs and gather our drunk asses up and go to the pool.

·   ·   ·   ·   ·

A few hours later, ribs sore from laughing, I flop myself down on a pool lounge next to Larry. I'm not sure how much I've had to drink, but I'm pretty sure the three of us cleaned out the mini bar.

"You know you're drunk," Larry informs me.

I lean back into the lounger and close my eyes. "My first time. And it didn't even hurt." When I open them, Larry's sitting on the edge of my chair, looking at me intensely.

And then without any kind of warm up or conversation, he's kissing me. And all of a sudden in the middle of this, I slowly uncoil inside. A wave of heat overwhelms me and then the nausea and bile begin to rise. I push away just in time before I vomit all over the lounger and all over the concrete next to me.

I should know better than to kiss a gay boy. Isn't this what happened last time I tried?

·   ·   ·   ·   ·

I open my eyes and am unsure of where I am. My eyes travel the ceiling above me and then circle down to the bed. I try to move my arms, but they are very heavy. Then I look to the side and sitting on the edge of the bed is Peter. That's when I remember everything. The kiss. The vomit. The falling down onto Larry. The cleaning up my own vomit. The dragging myself, crying up to the room. The boys behind me. Then just collapsing into the bed.

"Peter?" I ask him. My mouth tastes gross and yeasty.

"Hey." He smooths my hair and smiles. His eyes are glassy and red. I know from experience with Barb that you can stay drunk long after you've finished your last drop.

"Peter," I whisper. "I'm so sorry. I didn't mean anything—"

"It's fine. Gay test my ass."

Just then the bathroom door opens. Larry stumbles out and flops onto the bed next to me.

"Sorry, Maddie. Peter," he mumbles into the pillow.

"It's okay," I say to the back of his head.

Larry turns and all of the sudden he bursts into tears.

I struggle to sit up. Everything is spinning. I touch his back. "Hey. It's fine. People do stupid shit when they're drunk. Believe me, I've seen that about a million times."

Peter doesn't make a move to comfort Larry.

Larry wipes his nose into the pillow. "I've never kissed anyone." He makes a face like he doesn't want to cry again. "I lied to you, Peter. All I've ever heard about sex is that I better not do it or I'm going to hell. Christianity doesn't really make being any sexuality easy."

"But you seem," Peter searches for the right word, but then changes his mind and just says, "like you know so much."

"No, I really don't. I just read a lot," Larry tells him.

We all look at each other. Then I get a brilliant idea.

"I think you should all go brush your teeth. Maybe even shower. Then you need another gay test." I pause for dramatic effect. "One with Peter."

I haven't been able to read Peter. He's almost indifferent...except now. There's a look across his face that I've never seen. Not with Jack. Not with me.

Without a word Peter gets up and goes to the bathroom. Larry and I flip the TV on like a couple of normal teenagers hanging out in a hotel room. Five minutes later, Peter comes out with wet hair and smelling of scope.

Then Larry goes wordlessly into the bathroom. Peter lies next to me on my bed and puts his arm around me. I lie on his chest. We don't talk either. Ten minutes later, out comes Larry. Spicy sweet cologne fills the room. My turn. I go to the bathroom and take a good half hour. I scrub every part of my body and wash my hair three times. I even shave my legs. By the time I'm done I am practically sober and wondering if I should get my own room now.

When I open the door, Peter and Larry lie on the bed facing each other, talking quietly. No need for a gay test after all.

Time to call Justin again.

•　　•　　•　　•　　•

"Maddie."

"Hi."

"Where are you? Are you here already?"

My heart flutters.

"We should be there tomorrow night. I just wanted to let you know." So lame sounding...

"That's great. Cool, um...I'm probably about an hour from where your grandmother is. We can meet for lunch at my uncle's restaurant. It's right in Fishermen's Wharf."

God...he plans stuff too. So much has changed.

"Sure." I turn away from Peter and Larry and walk into the bathroom. "That sounds good...that sounds great." I stare at myself in the bathroom mirror now...Deep bags in my eyes. I try to fluff my hair as I say, "I can't wait to see you." I close my eyes, hoping he says the right thing back.

"You have no idea how much I want to see you too."

I smile. "Good night, Justin."

"Good night, Maddie."

CHAPTER SEVEN
"YOU BE THE LOOKOUT."

After our excursion with alcohol, all the three of us wanted to do was sleep. We slept a full twelve hours, had lunch, then got back on the road and have been driving straight since.

I turn into my grandmother's condo complex. The condos are all white with green trim. Some of them have garages and all of them have a deck off the back that overlooks the ocean. The grass is a brilliant emerald green and perfectly manicured. The sun is a yellow object following alongside me as I drive.

Just as we are about to turn onto my grandmother's street, Larry says, "We should have flowers or something for Bubbie."

"You're right," I say.

"I know what we can do. Pull over to the side. Let me out for a second," Larry says.

"What are you doing?" I ask.

"Peter, come with me. Maddie, you stay in the car and be the lookout." Larry flashes a devilish smile at me.

I watch them run down to an island of land with a garden of yellow, purple, and white flowers that separates the road we are on with the road that leads to Bubbie's condo. Larry and Peter each take a side of the garden, and I watch them pick the flowers. I look behind me every few seconds, knowing the strict rules and regulations of the neighborhood. One time, Barb and I went on flower picking adventure...and promptly got caught by a very crusty old man. I pull my legs up and lean into the window watching.

When they meet in the middle of the garden, almost head to head, they stop, still each holding a full bouquet. Larry stands all the way up and then Peter. They stand there for a minute, and it doesn't look like either one of them are saying anything. Larry moves closer. They are exactly the same height. Peter moves his hand as if he is going to touch Larry's arm, but it's Larry who puts his hand right up to Peter's face and pulls him close. They both still have the flowers and still hold them while they kiss. It kind of makes me think of a wedding. I don't turn away when they kiss, and my heart is full for them. They linger after the kiss but then seem to be laughing and looking around as if worried someone might see them. Then Larry grabs the flowers Peter is holding and puts them all together. They dart back to the car and open the door, breathless and smiling.

Peter puts the flowers in my face and says, "This good enough?"

I nod my head and grab the bouquets.

"They're perfect," I tell him.

. . . . .

"Maddie!"

"Bubbie!"

I'm lost in arms and kisses, enveloped in a lilac and cinnamon with a hint of mint scent that's not her familiar smell. Her silky purple scarf tied around her head brushes my cheek. She hears me sniff her neck and holds me at arm's length. "Joyce has me on all kinds of aromatherapy to help with the chemo side effects. Some of the stuff smells funny!" She wrinkles her nose.

"Oh, I like this smell," I tell her, anything that helps. "Now you're having side effects?"

"Not really. She says it's preventative...along with all the herbs and vitamins she's has me taking...and various voodoo doctors.

"Voodoo doctors?"

She shakes her head but smiles. "She's coming for dinner tonight. I'll have her explain it to you."

"Peter!" Bubbie turns to him as he comes behind me with his suitcase in one hand and my enormous rolling duffle in the other. She wraps her arms around his neck and they kiss each other's cheeks.

Larry is a few steps behind him.

"Bubbie, this is our friend Larry. Larry this is my Bubbie, Helen." Larry hands her the enormous yellow, white, and purple makeshift bouquet.

Bubbie takes it and smiles. "Fresh cut? Hmm, these look very similar to the community garden down the street."

We look at each other.

"Never mind. They're beautiful." She touches Larry's arm and then looks at all of us. "Let's get you all settled in," she says.

Bubbie tells us to figure out the sleeping arrangements. There is one spare bedroom, where Barb and I usually stay, and a fold out couch in the living room. I make the decision to have the fold out couch, and I give them the bedroom, which had two single beds in it. Both Larry and Peter are almost irritatingly happy.

Larry and Peter pass out on the couch and Bubbie and I go down to the beach to take a walk before Joyce arrives for dinner. In typical San Francisco weather, the temperature is cooler than what the thermometer reads. Luckily, we brought thick afghans that Bubbie got from a recent yoga retreat.

We settle on the sand up by some tall grass and she tucks her legs into a Buddha like position and wraps the afghan around her whole body. I stare at her profile. She closes her eyes and breathes in deeply.

After a long silence she says, "You know, I feel pretty good still."

I pull the afghan around me tightly.

Her hand goes to the scarf tied around her hair for a moment. "But I'm afraid of when I won't. Not my hair falling out. Now it's just one less thing to think about." She smiles, but it's tight. "The side effects of chemo can be brutal, unless you take all those pills to counteract the side effects and then those have side effects."

I want to tell her not to worry because I'll take care of her.

"But enough about me. Everything is about me lately, and it's tiresome. Tell me about you. I barely got to talk to you at graduation. The last we talked about you, you and Sean had broken up, prom was fun with Peter, and you were all set for Emerson."

For a moment, I see myself telling her my plans, and I see her looking relieved. But I know that's just the Maddie version. The reality version won't go like my fantasy.

"Justin's in San Francisco." I think I levitated at the end of the sentence.

"Really?"

"Really! He's staying with his uncle who owns this new pizza restaurant down on the wharf. It's called Big Tony's or something?"

"Big Tony is your Justin's uncle?" Bubbie laughs. "No kidding? Joyce and I go there practically every Friday night. Justin will be working there?"

"Yeah and he said something about taking some art classes."

"Oh the San Francisco Art Institute is a great place for art classes. Joyce and I took a few watercolor classes there. I was terrible of course. I should stick to writing!" Then she stops smiling. "Not that I've written anything in a year."

I reach out and touch her arm, although it's covered in blanket. "You will Bub. When this is all over."

"I hope so," she whispers. "Anyway, so Justin. This is a big deal. A very big deal." She flashes me a knowing smile.

"Yeah, it is," I admit.

We watch the surf for a few minutes and then I have to ask her:

"What, exactly is the game plan?" I pull the afghan around my shoulders. "Your chemo schedule and everything?"

"That's just what your mom asked me this morning! Speaking of, you better call her tonight." She adjusts the afghan around her shoulders. "Chemo is, "she knocks on her head, "not that bad. I do have a prescription for some medical marijuana." She shakes her head. "Not sure how that works with my sobriety but not an issue right now."

"Is chemo every day?"

"It's every other day right now and not interfering with work, but I know that as the stuff settles into my system, I might feel crappy, even with Joyce's magic potions. Luckily, I'm only teaching in the first summer session." She studies my face. "I want to do our usual hike through Muir woods. I want to walk across the Golden Gate bridge like we've talked about but never done together." She playfully gives me a little push. "But don't you dare make me run!"

"Are you sure?"

"Yes, until I don't feel like it. I want to live my life normally, fully!"

I take a deep breath. My conscience tugging me about not telling her the whole truth and knowing that it's only a matter of time before my mother spills it anyway.

I push the afghan off of myself and stretch my arms out in back of me. "I need to tell you something," I begin.

Without looking at me and still calm and serene, she says, "I already know. Just waiting for you to tell me yourself."

But before I can say anything else I hear, "Hey, Helen! Helen, is that Maddie with you! Oh, Maddie so good to see you, sweetie."

Saved by Joyce.

"This isn't finished," Bubbie says giving me the look reserved for things like not telling her everything. But then she reaches over and puts her arms around me.

"You are very sweet, though, to want to take care of me," she says rocking me close, and I bury my face into her cinnamon smelling neck, feel the cool silk of her scarf, happy to be in California.

CHAPTER EIGHT
"SCARED YOU PRETTY BAD!"

The next morning, I roll out of the pull-out couch at 10:30. My mouth is dry and pasty. I walk through the living room and the hallway and reach the kitchen where Larry stands at the stove making scrambled eggs...or egg whites. It's hard to tell from my bleary-eyed position in the doorway. He has an apron on that has a picture of a naked woman sitting in the lotus position.

"Good morning, sunshine!"

"Bubbie is already rubbing off on you." I yawn. "Where's everyone?"

"Sleeping...Not Helen. She was out in her garden, and I think she's in the shower now.

I walk in and sit at the table. "God, I feel like shit. So tired." I yawn again.

"Get some energy because lover boy called." Larry flashes his impish smile. "You left your phone in the living room, and I saw his name flash about three times. Once last night after you went to bed and twice this morning."

I open my mouth to respond when I hear soft padding footsteps behind me.

In walks Bubbie, looking scrubbed pink and healthy. She has small brimmed sun hat covering her head and her arm through Peter's, who looks equally robust.

"Golden Gate Park," Peter holds what looks like some tourist book on California in his hands. "Did you know it's all man-made?"

I know nothing about Golden Gate Park even though Bubbie used to take me there when I was little.

"Every time Maddie visits we promise to take a walk across the bridge. It's not very long."

"Let's do it today." Peter closes the book and sits next to me.

"I think we should all spend the day on the beach," Larry says sliding eggs onto one of the four plates he has on the counter.

"June is still cold for the beach in San Francisco," Bubbie says. "But I'm all for bundling up and hanging out. I have some papers to correct."

"What about the Golden Gate Park?" Peter asks.

Larry walks over and serves Peter first. "We have three weeks here. We'll get to it, promise." He strokes his head like they've been together for years, and Peter melts right in front of us.

"Get a room and not in my Bubbie's apartment!"

We all laugh, including Bubbie.

We eat breakfast, which is way better than I expected from Larry. The beach wins over the park because, quite frankly, we are all exhausted from the trip. As we pack towels and lotion, Bubbie goes to the bathroom leaving me with Peter and Larry.

"I gotta say, she doesn't seem sick."

"I know," I say.

"You may not have a good excuse to stay in San Fran." Peter adds.

"Oh, Jesus!" From the bathroom, Bubbie yelps out.

We all stop talking.

"Oh shit!" and this is from my grandmother who rarely uses English swear words as Yiddish swearing is more emphatic according to her.

We all rush to the half bathroom in the hallway.

"Bubbie?" I knock on the door.

"Everything all right in there?" There's no trace of witty Larry on his face.

I hear the toilet flush and the sink turn on. The three of us stand mouths open waiting.

Then the door opens. Bubbie, her bald head smooth and shiny, looks aggravated like she just realized she left a bag of groceries at the supermarket and has to go back. But what she says is, "I gotta call my doctor. There's blood."

•   •   •   •   •

Bubbie is in her bedroom with the door closed, on the phone with her doctor. We all sit frozen on the couch. A box of tissues half on my lap and half on Peters. No one is crying, but for some reason I grabbed the box when we went to sit down and wait for Bubbie to call her doctor. I tear a tissue into bits and make small piles on my lap. I stare at the Matisse poster of three women dancing in a circle on the wall.

Then my phone buzzes on the coffee table. Larry's face brightens, and I feel mine get warm.

When I look at the caller ID, it's "Mom".

She always has impeccable timing.

"You should answer it," Peter says.

I shake my head and Larry nods. "Not yet. Call her later."

I let it keep ringing and each buzz causes the inside of my body to tighten up, particularly my chest. Peter grabs my hand. When it stops, we all get quiet. Waiting.

.   .   .   .   .

When Bubbie finally opens the door of her bedroom, her eyes are red, but she looks relatively calm. Her scarf is back on.

"The doctor can see me at two."

"We'll all go," Larry says.

After changing back to land clothes, we file into Larry's car, top up not down. In the backseat with Bubbie, I hold her hand and with my other one I grip my phone. Justin has called, yet again.

"Call him, sweetie. I'm not dying or anything."

She smiles, but I don't. I just look out the window. "Not now."

.   .   .   .   .

A half hour later the four of us are sitting in the waiting room of Dr. Schlosberg, a premier cancer specialist in the Bay area. We sit tightly, not reading the various collections of *National Geographic*, *Vanity Fair*, and *Ladies Home Journal*. I haven't let go of Bubbie's hand, Larry has his arm on

Peter's chair, and Peter has his arm around me.

A woman comes out of the closed door wearing pink doggie scrubs. "Helen Kurland?"

"I'll come with you," I say to Bubbie.

"No, honey. You guys wait here." She gets up and pats my knee. "I'll be fine."

Larry moves to sit on the other side of me. He puts his hand in mine and says, "As soon as we leave, you need to call Justin."

Peter leans in and adds, "He's called me three times now. You have to call him back."

"We may be here a while. You could go call him out there."

"Guys," my throat is tight. "Please, stop. "I glance around at the other people in the waiting room, most of which are staring dully at the flat screen TV that blares CNN news about yet another conflict in the Middle East

We sit in silence, but I untwine myself from them both. After fifteen minutes of staring at the spotless blue carpet, I stand up.

They both look at me hopeful, but I shake my head. "Going to get a soda."

I push open the swinging door to the main entrance of the building a little more roughly than I meant to. My face gets hot as I walk into the wide hallway and search for vending machine.

Then my phone. Rings.

My stomach clenches and my heart grows huge and thudding.

Frankly I've had too much therapy to not know that despite Bubbie's situation now and in general, it has nothing to do with why I'm not calling Justin back. Because the only thing stopping me is me.

I answer it.

"Hi."

"Are you here?"

I laugh. "Yes. Actually, I'm at the doctor's."

"Is Bubbie okay?"

I don't speak for at least a solid minute and the tears collect silently in my lower lids.

He finally says. "I can come sit with you."

I find my voice, although it's shaky. "No, no. I haven't seen you in a long time, and I don't want our great reunion to be in a friggin' hospital."

I hear him make a kind of frustrated noise. "Will you call me, though? As soon as you hear something? As soon as you leave? Or if you're staying, call me."

"I'll call you," I tell him. "Promise."

·　·　·　·　·

"Pass me the parmesan cheese—"

"Hand me the salt—"

"Can I have that spicy pepper stuff?"

"Hand me a napkin, hon, will you?"

"Can I get anybody anything?" Uncle Tony, an *über* Italian man with curly salt and pepper hair that has the sheen of a well-oiled pair of black shoes, claps his hands together and grins. "Anybody want some more of those little necks? We got plenty!"

"Me!" Peter swipes the grease from his lips. Even health nut Larry nods his head.

"One more round of little necks coming!" Then he leans down and says not so quietly to Justin, "You told me Maddie was gorgeous, but you forgot to mention her grandmother." I watch Bubbie stop chewing and look over at Tony. He winks.

And she winks back.

After he disappears through the double red doors of the kitchen Bubbie says, "Mmmm, this is so good. Can we do this after every impromptu colonoscopy?"

"They gave you a colonoscopy?"

I grab the napkins and hand them to Bubbie and say to Justin, "No. A little colon cancer humor."

He cracks his adorable but kind of mischievous smile, his blue eyes definitely greyer then I remember. Do eyes change as you get older or had I never really looked carefully?

That I am sitting thigh to thigh in a cozy booth next to him, that I smell this unfamiliar soap mixed with guy deodorant scent, that I feel his breath on my cheek when he laughs, these are all tiny details that imprint themselves on me as we eat dinner. Admittedly the euphoria of finding out that Bubbie is fine, that this might just be the first good summer I've had in years, these are all my thoughts as I pull a blob of cheese from my pizza and pop it in my mouth.

It turns out, the blood she saw in her stool was just from her fastidious hygiene habits. And it turns out, Justin while on the phone with me, was on his way ...he had already talked to Peter. Now we were back in town at Big Tony's Pizzeria, enjoying my favorite mushroom and cheese. New York style, floppy and big so you can fold it. Yum.

My reunion with Justin wasn't filled with swelling classical music, and I wasn't dressed in my flowing best. But it was still pretty good. Because as soon as I hung up the phone and turned around, he was walking through the double doors of the building. And thanks to surprising me there was no time to stop myself from running into his arms.

It was pretty awesome.

And now, laughing with some of my most favorite people in the world all together eating the best pizza ever, I declare to myself that I will finally, *finally* have a good summer.

·　　·　　·　　·　　·

Right before bed that night I walk into Bubbie's room. She's reading a gardening magazine. Her glasses are on the end of her nose and she's wearing a soft blue cotton scarf on her head.

"Scared you pretty bad today, huh?" She says.

"Yeah," I say climbing on the bed and sitting cross-legged.

"Scared myself, too." She closes her magazine. I can faintly hear Peter and Larry in the bedroom down the hall.

"But I realize something tonight." She touches my hand. "Sitting with you all at dinner, flirting with Mr. Uncle Tony, watching you moon over Justin, I'd rather have three great months, weeks, or days left than three horrible, sick years."

I'm not sure what she means, so I just wait for more.

"The chemo is not easy." Is that an ironic smile across her face? "I've managed because of medical marijuana. I actually have been using that prescription, which goes against everything in my being. But I know that there are so many more months of chemo. Joyce tried to get an herbal regimen together that could replace the pot, but it didn't cut the debilitating nausea, the itching, or the metal taste in my mouth." She looks away. "I didn't want to tell you and your mom and Barb how bad the side effects were...They were really bad just before your graduation. In fact, just two days before is when I—" she chuckles, "smoked my first joint for the first time in years. I needed to get relief fast. The doctors were worried about how much weight I had lost from not being able to eat much. I could barely function at work. But you know, as soon as the drugs hit my system, no more nausea." She plays with the fringe of the Indian blanket that's across her lap. "But that feeling scared me. I've been sober a long time, but it's not something I take for granted."

I take in each of these revelations bite by bite and then put together the entire elephant...

I can't even find the words to say what's in my head. "Does this mean...?"

"I'm not sure what it means. Tomorrow is chemo and that's what I do right after." She laughs wryly. "Light up. Sometimes even as the poison is finishing up hitting my bloodstream. There's a bunch of cancer people hooked up to IVs getting high."

"I'll tell you...if I don't die from colon cancer, I might die from lung cancer." She wrinkles her nose.

"What about just eating it, in like a brownie or something?"

"And what do you know about pot brownies?"

"Saw something about them on a reality show." I give her a gentle push. "Bubbie, you really think I would smoke a joint?"

"Everyone experiments."

"True."

"The problem with the pills or brownies is the relief isn't as strong or immediate...I don't know. But I just feel like I might want to try alternatives to chemo and smoking weed." The look she throws my way reminds me so much of my mother that I feel another stab of guilt for not calling her.

And because my mother can actually channel her guilt through phone lines, guilt is so strong, my phone buzzes in my pocket and it's her, I know this before I even look at it.

I press the call button. Bubbie watches me.

"Hi, Mom."

"Madeline, I've been calling you."

"I know—"

"Your father and I—"

"Hi, sweetie!"

"Hi, Dad."

"Listen, we were a little worried."

"A little? I was about to call the police! And Bubbie didn't answer her cell either."

I choose each word carefully. "We had a busy day...and yesterday I was kind of wiped out from the drive. Things are good."

"Good! Is the weather nice?"

I put my hand to my forehead. "Yeah, Dad, the weather is good."

"Is that car holding up? Not sure about those convertibles on long drives." My father knows nothing about cars, and it's Mom who always gets the oil changed or the tires rotated.

"How's Bubbie?" At this point Bubbie and I are almost ear-to-ear with the phone between us. Her scarf brushes my cheek.

"She's—" Bubbie shakes her head and I continue, "She's good, Mom."

"I mean how does she seem? Are her spirits up? Because I noticed at graduation—"

My mother used to be the queen of denial and excuses and then my sister happened and now she can smell what you feel even thousands of miles away.

That's when Bubbie takes the phone, "Hi, honey. I'm doing fine. Really. Maddie is taking me to chemo tomorrow."

I am?

She nods at me.

I guess...I am.

I listen to Bubbie carefully reassure my mother some more without totally out and out lying.

Before I kiss her good night, Bubbie says to me, "Tomorrow, be ready at eight. Chemo and then off to my office to turn in my final grades for the summer session. I'm going to need you because I will be pretty tired and nauseous." She smiles and strokes my hair. "I'm going to try this, as Joyce says, 'balls out' No pot after."

I cover my hand with my mouth. Cancer has made my Bubbie have a toilet mouth...and I kind of like it.

CHAPTER NINE
BALLS OUT

I open the car door with my free hand. The other one is holding Bubbie's elbow.

"Ugh..." She closes her eyes as I guide her into the front seat. While I pull the seat belt across her lap, she moans more. Her small knit cap is slightly crooked. I reach out to adjust it.

"Do you need the bag?" As in vomit bag. They give you free ones, like a lollypop after the doctor, on your way out of chemo.

She shakes her head.

I click the belt in and pause, "Bubbie, are you sure that you don't want to smoke a little bit?"

She shakes her head with her hand over her mouth.

I sigh. "Joyce is meeting us at the house with some kind of magic potion."

Bubbie tries to laugh. Her eyes still closed and her hand still over her mouth.

I place a vomit bag the color of vomit onto her lap then get in and turn the car on.

•   •   •   •   •

When I get her home, I put her to bed with a bucket by her side. Larry and Peter ask me if they can help, but there's nothing any of us can do. They're going to take the trip to Golden Gate park and stay overnight at a hotel, but only after I reassure them that I won't sit here by myself, and yes, I will call Justin back (he called while we were at the hospital, but it felt really wrong to answer the phone while my grandmother was barfing).

Before I leave the room, she grabs my hand and says, "Thank you, sweetie, for taking me today and for holding my hair when I vomited."

I squeeze her hand and swallow the urge to ask her once again if she wants to take some of the marijuana pills. She made me throw it out, but all I did was put it in my suitcase, just in case.

·   ·   ·   ·   ·

Justin and I have been playing phone tag all evening. He's at work until eleven. The urge to walk down to the wharf is strong, but Joyce called and asked if she could come by.

Bubbie is still sleeping when Joyce gently taps on the door at five. When I open the door, she looks about as good as my grandmother. I invite her in with the ulterior motive of getting her in on my campaign to get Bubbie high.

·   ·   ·   ·   ·

We sit together on the couch in the living room with mugs of cinnamon apple tea.

"So." We both say.

She smiles at me. "Go ahead, honey."

"No, you," I don't know how to begin this.

She fluffs her curly hair but not in a primping way. She folds her hands in her lap. "There's something I want to discuss with you."

Great minds think alike.

"Actually, there's something I need to discuss with you too, but you go first. Maybe it's the same thing."

She shakes her head. "I don't think so."

I feel my face do a free fall. I put my mug on the coffee table.

"There's this place, up in Sausalito—"

"A place?"

"Yes, sweetie. The ACT."

"The ACT?"

"Alternative Cancer Therapy center of Sausalito."

"Alternative...?"

"They offer all kinds of different treatments for cancer." She reaches into her purse and pulls out a pamphlet. It has pictures of people all ages and races on the beach, smiling like it's summer camp. She hands it to me. "Look, I wasn't thrilled about all this when Helen brought it up to me."

"Brought it up to you?" Apparently, all I can do is parrot things back now.

"Yes, she brought it up to me a few weeks ago. And I want you to know I told her it was crazy and that we didn't exactly have time on our side time to dilly-dally with *mishegas*. We needed to kill this thing...balls out!" She's smiling at me.

I don't smile back.

"I admit I was the one to say let's investigate some other ways to deal with the side effects, but I never ever once told her she should stop the chemo or stop the marijuana. That was all her. I want her to do everything, all at the same time. Because," her voice catches. "I can't lose my best friend, my sister, my partner."

I hand her the box of tissues and take one for myself.

We cry separately for a moment.

"The deal is that your grandmother has been preparing for this, and she wants to do it now."

"How do you know? She hasn't mentioned anything to me."

"She signed the paper work this week, just on Monday." Joyce takes another tissue and dabs the corner of eyes, which have little streaks of eyeliner bleed down. "And they told her about a week until they could take her."

"I don't understand. Last night she told me 'balls out' let's go ahead and do this chemo. She just didn't want to smoke the weed after." I snatch a tissue even though I'm not crying any more.

"My guess is that she did that for you, honey, so you could see how bad the chemo was how awful it made her feel so that maybe you would understand."

"I don't understand shit!" I grip the tissue in my fist. "She would be fine with the chemo if she would just get over it and smoke the weed!"

Joyce cringes.

"All I know is that my Bubbie, my so-called honest, truth-telling, AA-touting Bubbie has been lying to me about a bunch of stuff with this cancer, and I can't figure out why she won't just tell me the friggin' truth, herself?" I yell and throw my hands up, the balled-up tissue flying out.

Joyce doesn't say anything. She just sits and looks at me without a crack of a smile or a whiff of sympathy.

"Helen was definitely going to tell you, Maddie. I just beat her to the punch." Joyce sips her tea but keeps her eyes on me. "How much do you know about your grandmother's addictions?"

"She's an alcoholic, a recovering alcoholic." It's a textbook answer and one that I say in a normal voice.

"Yes. But she's also a drug addict."

Bubbie was a hippy in the sixties, and I know she smoked "grass" as she called it back then. But drug addict?

"After she was clean for twenty years, she had a relapse, but it wasn't with alcohol. Pills. Then marijuana. Then both."

I did the math quickly in my head. Her relapse was only three years ago...just before my sister's wedding. Just before she and my mom mended their very broken fences.

"Helen's fear about becoming addicted to pot is real. I dismissed it at first, but she's serious. The fact that she went to chemo without using anything shows me she is intent on not doing the medical marijuana."

I can't think of any reply to this that would make anything different.

"I don't understand why she wouldn't want to chemo though." I swallow more tears to prepare for the next part of what I am saying. "Without it she will die and with it she will possibly live."

"Not if the side effects kill her." Joyce's eyes flash at me. "You see her. This is what it will be like every day she has chemo and the plan is to increase it to every day for the last three weeks of treatment."

"But the anti-nausea pills—"

"Don't work for her—"

"What about a feeding tube when she can't eat?" I cross my arms.

"Maddie."

I look up at the staircase. Bubbie.

"How are you feeling, Helen?" Joyce stands up and tries to make her face calm.

"Horrendous." Her head is uncovered, and she looks smaller and younger. She takes a step holding the railing, stops and then just sits down and puts her head in her hand for a minute. Now I stand up and make my way to her, but she looks over at me and says, "Honey, it's okay. I just need to try and eat something, but I came down to tell you that I'm done and I tried it and maybe it doesn't look like I'm trying hard enough. But this is my life, my body, and my choice. I don't like what chemo does to me because other than another tumor pressing into my stomach, I feel fine. I don't feel sick. I won't do any more chemicals to this body." She puts her hand to her mouth like she's going to throw up.

Joyce is at her side faster than I thought she was capable of moving. I watch her help Bubbie stand up and walk her back to her room. I just stay where I am.

· · · · ·

Joyce comes down about a half hour later. I've been sitting holding my cell phone, debating calling Justin or my mother.

"They can take her now."

"Now?"

"Now."

I scratch my forearm, which doesn't itch. Then I cross and uncross my legs. "For how long?"

Joyce sits next to me her voice is calm and soft. "They'd like to keep her for a while, and if she seems to be improving, she will come back home and just go for treatments as a day patient."

"Joyce." I take an impatient breath. "For how long?"

"I don't know," she says quietly. "Probably a week and then outpatient treatment."

I don't want her to go. I just got here. I want her to smoke the weed and do the chemo. That's what the doctors say will work. This other shit. This hocus-pocus.

But all I can actually say to Joyce is, "Who's paying for this? Not health insurance." Although my knowledge of health insurance is similar to my knowledge about alternatives to cancer treatment: nil.

Joyce looks away, then down at the rings on her finger, and then looks at me with red eyes and a tired face. "Don't worry about that. She's figured that out."

I sigh and look out the window. The trees in the front of the house sway.

Joyce reaches out and takes my hand in hers, but I keep mine limp. "Maddie, you have to accept her decision."

.   .   .   .   .

11:15. I'm still on the couch, now with a reading lamp on and an unopened copy of *Writer's & Poets* on my lap. My hand has a pen in it, and my journal is open, but nothing is written.

I haven't written a thing since I finished the book for school.

Of course, writer's block pales in comparison to Cancer.

You can't die from Writer's Block...I don't think. Or maybe that will bring the cancer on for me. I've also spent some of the last few hours online researching alternatives for cancer treatment, and there's several real, well-known, non-hocus pocus doctors that attribute cancer to stress. And cell phones. But that's another anxiety to panic over at another time.

I'm, once again, in pure Maddie Hickman fashion, steeped in self-pity.

And that one, I do write down in my journal. Hooray. I close it up and tuck the pen in the side of it, my potential cancer is cured.

My phone buzzes next to me on the coffee table, and Justin's name is illuminated in the semi darkness.

Before he can get his hello out, I tell him everything.

"She should talk to my uncle. You know he beat prostate cancer. Think it was stage three or something. It was pretty bad. He did chemo and radiation, I'm pretty sure. Maybe she needs to talk to someone outside of the family or the situation, you know?"

I want to reach into the phone and kiss him, but we technically haven't even been on a date yet.

"I want to see you," I blurt out.

"Me too. I want to see you, now. Right now."

"Have you left work yet?"

"Leaving now. I can just stop by."

"What are you doing tomorrow?"

"I work until five."

"Come over for dinner," I close my eyes and pray he says yes.

"Yes," I open my eyes and my cheeks hurt from smiling

"I'll bring pizza."

We sit in silence and it's comfortable like when we were dating we would sit in silence on the phone and watch TV.

"But can't I come see you now?"

I catch myself in the reflection of the window and see my hair piled in tangles on my head, and I know my eyes and nose are puffy.

"No, I mean I want you to, but you won't be able to stay long."

"So, what?"

"I'm all puffy from crying—"

"And that matters because I'm taking you to prom?"

My nose is *really* puffy. I touch my hair. A mess.

"You're right. It doesn't matter."

.   .   .   .   .

"Hi." Blue grey eyes. Thick black lashes. I put my hand on the door to steady myself.

"Hi." I breathe.

"Everyone asleep?" He takes a step towards me.

"Yeah, Peter and Larry are gone till tomorrow."

"Want to come outside or do you want me to come in?"

"Oh, yeah. Um, hold on. Let me come out there." I reach around and make sure the door is unlocked, and then I slide on my flip-flops.

I step outside, the air smells wet and salty like the ocean that's nearby. Without any kind of warning, Justin pulls me into him and holds me tight. "I couldn't do this yesterday. It's all I've been thinking about," he says into the top of my head.

His hands move up and down my back, leaving a trail of heat. My arms wind around his neck and my fingertips brush the soft ends of his hair. Running my hands through it might be a little too forward. We linger in the embrace, I can faintly hear the waves crashing from the beach that's behind the condos.

Justin moves his head so that it's tucked into my neck and I can ever so lightly feel his lips on my skin. Goose bumps trickle down my arms. Please don't let me go, I pray silently. Even though in my fantasy we make out and rip our clothes off when we first see each other, that doesn't seem right. I want him to hold me and me to hold him and to be in this moment.

Then he sighs, his breath against my cheek. "I wish I could stay, but Uncle Tony is kind of insane when I'm home too late."

I let my arms drop and say, "Yeah."

We break apart but leave only inches between our bodies. He meets my gaze. Really, I'm gazing at him, I can feel it. We both laugh like we're embarrassed. He touches my arm and moves back in.

He drops his arm and smiles crookedly shaking his head. "Man, is it ever not intense with us?"

"Nope," I say grinning.

He grins back.

We hug again. But I do wonder, when are we going to get that first kiss?

"See you tomorrow."

"Tomorrow."

"Bye."

I watch him walk to his car, savoring the back of his head, his t-shirt that reads, in red letters, Big Tony's Pizzeria. I watch his butt, hard to really see in his baggy khakis. I think about when I might be able to touch his butt.

He turns around and catches me staring and smiles like he knows.

I know he knows, and I smile back.

•   •   •   •   •

I turn over and open my eyes. The shades are still up, I forgot to pull them down last night. I fell asleep so quickly, I look down and see that I didn't even change my clothes.

Justin.

I sniff my arms and pull up my shirt and smell it to see if his scent is there. Faintly, I smell pizza and deodorant and soap and this other good smell, but I think I'm imagining it all.

I reach down on the floor without sitting up and feel for my journal. The pen is still stuck to it. I sit up and open it to yesterday's single sentence entry. I print today's date, at least what I think it is, and then I begin to write:

How can two totally opposite things be happening to me at the same time? Death. Love. Maybe they aren't opposite.

I stop writing, sad that this tiny spark flickered out by the end of the last word. But it's still better than yesterday, two sentences today.

Baby steps...Bubbie would say.

•   •   •   •   •

I stand in the kitchen holding a mug of coffee. Bubbie and Joyce are at the kitchen table with a map spread out and my grandmother's laptop open. They hunch over it like they are planning a camping trip or a girls' weekend to a yoga retreat.

"You'll have yoga classes every morning and massage and acupuncture treatments several times a week." Her eyes dart back and forth as she reads. "Patients begin with a detox and cleanse to jumpstart the healing process." She clicks on something and is silent, then she reads, "Most tumors contain multiple drug resistant cells which means that the chemo is not effective on these cells, yes they will kill the other cells in the tumor, but you will still have those drug resistant cells. What does that mean? That the cancer can still spread. This is why if your cancer is reoccurring and chemo will be less effective." Joyce pauses and looks up at me from the map. I turn away and reach for the coffee pot for a refill.

"And," Bubbie adds, "The real deal with cancer, especially reoccurring, is that I have to get treatments that will get rid of all the bad cells, not just some." She reaches over Joyce and turns the laptop to her and begins to type. "There's this vitamin C therapy and there's also Angiogenesis therapy which actually stops the blood vessels from growing in the tumors. But the conventional Angiogenesis treatments doctors use can actually cause the blood vessels to grow."

I take a huge gulp of coffee. Too hot! I choke.

They are engrossed in the damn website and don't even turn to look at me. I spit coffee into the sink and then wipe my mouth with a paper towel. I sigh audibly but still no response.

"Maddie, can you make some of that new tea Joyce brought?"

"Sure." I put the teakettle on.

Then the doorbell rings.

No one moves. "Maybe it's Peter and Larry?" I say this out loud, but they still don't respond. I look at the clock on the stove it's only eight o'clock. They aren't even up yet probably.

I walk to the door and open it and in front of me are two people wearing black tight t-shirts that say Big Tony's Pizzeria: NYC Style Pizza in the Bay Area with a curly haired Italian guy who looks deceptively like Tony in a chef outfit holding a huge pizza in one hand. New t-shirts.

I hear the chairs scrape behind me.

"Hi, ladies! You are all looking lovely this morning, may I say." Tony smiles at me, and then peers around to Bubbie and gives a little wave.

I look at Justin and he smiles and mouths hi. I say hi back.

"Come in, gentleman," Bubbie says, standing up and touching the purple knit cap on her head.

"We have coffee," Joyce is all flirts and smiles. "and I brought some really lovely mint and aloe tea."

Tony laughs deep and says, "That sounds like some kind of face cream or something. No thanks, ladies. Actually, Helen thought I could talk with you for a moment this beautiful morning. Can we go somewhere?" He glances at Joyce.

Bubbie wipes her clean hands on her jeans and says, "Sure, absolutely. Would you like to come out to the garden? It's really wonderful in the morning out there."

"That sounds fantastic! "

As soon as they leave out the backdoor sliders, Justin says to me, "I told him everything, and the next thing I knew we were on our way to your house."

Joyce folds the map up and closes the laptop.

"He's a prostate cancer survivor." Justin says this to Joyce, but she is engrossed in folding the map and straightening the napkin holder on the table.

"He did chemo for almost a year and he's fine."

Joyce slams the map on the table. "I'm happy to hear that your uncle survived cancer. But if Maddie put you up to this to try and stop Helen," she shakes her head and looks at me. "You have to respect your grandmother's decisions. This is her life and her choice, not yours."

"Actually, it's my choice how I deal with it, and I'm not going down without a fight, a fight for my Bubbie, who means more to me than," I stop and press my fingers to my lips because I don't want to cry right this minute. "She means more to me than anyone else in my life, and so if I can try even just little bit, even if I totally fail I'm going to try to get her one last time to do the chemo. I mean why can't we do both treatments? Why can't we keep researching ways to deal with the side effects of the chemo? She doesn't want to smoke pot, fine. There are other medicines." I stop when I see that I'm not getting through to Joyce, she's tight lipped, pissed.

"You're right. It is your choice how you deal with it. But remember that at some point, you do have to let go and just be there for her. Just be her granddaughter."

The room is thick with awkwardness and tension. Justin moves closer to me and takes my hand. We sit at the table. Joyce joins us and none of us look at each other or say anything.

The sliders glide open and make the smack sound of shutting. We all stand up. Bubbie is red eyed, holding a tissue. Tony has his hand on the small of shoulder and is just as red eyed. Bubbie turns to Tony and reaches up they hug and pat each other's backs. It is a really private moment that the three of us are watching.

"Thank you, Tony. And I'm so happy that you are healthy."

He nods and wipes his eyes. "Thank you, Helen. Always good to trade war stories."

They laugh and hug again.

"My boy, we need to get to work. Have a nice day ladies and," He looks at Bubbie, "a safe trip."

She smiles and sniffles a little pressing her tissue to her nose.

It's hard to tell what's happened. Justin hugs me and puts his lips to my cheek. It's so distracting, it's our first kiss in a way. I forget about the rest of the people in the room. I forget about Cancer. I forget about my life being where it is, and yet I remember it all at the same time too, and it makes me grip Justin's arm tighter and press my lips to his cheek before we say goodbye.

.   .   .   .   .

"Just promise me, Bub, promise me that we will take that walk across the bridge?"

"Of course, sweetie. I'm coming back in two weeks. The day I come back we will take that walk." Then she whispers in my ear, "Please make up with Joyce. She tends to be a mother tiger about me. Go on."

I release my grip on Bubbie and turn to Joyce who is slamming the trunk shut with their bags inside.

"Joyce," I say.

She turns to me. "Maddie." Instantly I know we are fine. We are fine because we want the same thing, for Bubbie to live.

We hug goodbye. "I'll call Mom and give her the scoop," I tell Bubbie.

"Thank you," she says as they pull out of the driveway. "We will call you once we are settled."

I wave and yell, "Love you" as they drive away.

CHAPTER TEN
A DATE...FINALLY

Bubbie calls at 4 pm, sounding happy and excited. She says that I can even come visit her in a few days. Joyce tells me the place is amazing. And surprisingly the conversation with my mother goes well. "My mother is not one to change her mind. But that doesn't mean we can't try. I'll give her this week at this cancer spa and then I'll fly down there if I have to and schlep her myself to chemo." Gotta love Mom. And who knows, maybe Bubbie will change her mind. Maybe she will see that she can do both.

•　　•　　•　　•　　•

At 6 pm I light vanilla scented candles on the kitchen table, then set out four paper plates, napkins, cups, and utensils. I put the salad I made (hope Justin still loves olives and tomatoes) and a bottle of soda (does he still like Dr. Pepper?) on the table. I go back into the living room for the tenth time to reposition the pillows on the couch and re-rearrange the books on the coffee table. I check myself in the mirror above the fireplace four more times. I go in and out of the bathroom, brushing my hair and reapplying lip-gloss. I scrutinize my skin in both mirrors (because the lighting is different in each room) and check to see if the shampoo I used did, in fact, bring out my natural highlights. Maybe it's just the lighting but instead of a sort of dirty haystack blonde, I see some golden highlights.

I check my lip-gloss one final time, when the doorbell rings.

"Hi!" I say.

Fresh off their overnight, Larry and Peter cheek kiss and hug me.

"Everything all right with Helen?" Larry asks.

I nod and stand back to let them in. "She sounded happy when she called. I mean, I'm not thrilled but, you know."

"When can we visit her?" Peters asks walking into the house after Larry. "A few days."

Justin stands to the side holding roses in one hand and two pizza boxes (one smaller than the other). He leans in to kiss my cheek and whispers, "How are you?"

"Fine," I whisper back then say in a normal voice. "Do you want some help?"

He hands me the flowers. "You hold these."

I take the roses. They smell like a kiss, like the way it will feel when we finally kiss, oh god when will we finally kiss?

He puts the boxes on the kitchen table. Larry has a bottle of fake wine with him.

"This shit smells so good. Best pizza." Larry proclaims putting the fake bottle of wine on the table.

"Tony makes the sauce every morning himself...No one's allowed in the kitchen." Justin pulls a chair out and it makes a scraping sound.

Meanwhile, I'm shaking for some reason and busying myself with looking for a vase for the flowers. The guys continue chatting and I find a vase and fill it with water and put the flowers in. Then I try to open the pizza box, which is absurdly difficult. Larry saunters over holding a cup of soda. He whispers in my ear, "Just breathe. Trust me, Justin is a sure thing." I punch him in the arm and grumble, "Help me with this box." After we manage to open the pizza box, I pass out the pizza.

"Oh, shit," I say as I plop a piece onto Peter's place. I put the box down on the counter behind me. "I got some bread from that bakery down the street." I go to the oven, open it, and grab the bread—

"Fuck!" Fingers burning and face, too because of my f-bomb.

The guys leap up and swarm me.

"Cold water... put her hand... come here Maddie, put your hand in here." I feel first Justin's warm hand and then the sharp cold water on my fingertips.

"Here's some ice," this from Larry.

Peter has his hand on my shoulder, "Are you okay?"

I nod. Justin turns off the water. Larry gives me a bag of ice to hold, and they all steer me to the table.

"Sit."

And I do.

Larry pours me a glass of fake wine. "Pretend it's real." He puts it in my good hand. I drink.

I look at my hand. "I kind of felt like I was on one of those doctor shows, you guys were so fast."

Justin reaches for my hand and opens it up carefully. "It's just a little red. Think you'll live." He holds it for a beat longer and looks at me. I blush again. For a second, I think he might kiss it.

Larry clears his throat and says, "I propose a toast."

We all lift our glasses.

"To reunions."

I throw Larry a look, but he winks at me.

The placebo wine works because we pass pizza, bread, and salad around the table and eat and laugh. My fingers stop hurting. Towards the end of the meal, Larry turns on Bubbie's old "boombox" and adjusts the radio. Some old song I don't recognize comes on.

"I think we should all dance," he announces. "Peter, have you ever danced with a guy?"

Peter glances at Justin. But Justin just stands up and takes my hand. "Let's all dance."

At first, we laugh and goof around because the song is so cheesy. I tango and then dip with Justin, but then he spins me away and grabs Larry and they tango. This makes me crack up. Peter twirls me around and then I twirl him. And then...

Another old song comes on. Except this one I recognize.

Justin releases Larry from the half bear hug they found themselves in, and the whole mood of the room switches. Out of the corner of my eye, I see Larry take Peter's hand.

"Do you remember the last time we danced?" Justin is so close to me now I can gaze like a fool into his eyes.

"Yes." Why am I shaking?

"This was the song," he whispers, his lips next to my ear and his hands around my waist. "In my room. It's from one of those eighties, teen movies."

I nod into the crook of his neck, his skin against my lips.

"And we didn't talk. Just danced." He sighs, his breath warm in my ear.

We dance in silence and Justin squeezes me closer, so close I feel his heart and his muscles in his chest. It's the single best feeling, ever.

．　　．　　．　　．　　．

The guys hang out in the living room as I go back into the kitchen to put some coffee on and get dessert ready. Peter follows me. He helps me make the coffee and then says, "I really hope that you don't blow it."

"What!" I laugh but he's serious. "Why would I blow it?"

"I don't know...You're used to being miserable."

We look at each other for another minute before getting the cake and coffee.

．　　．　　．　　．　　．

At exactly 10 pm, Larry and Peter, because they are geniuses, tell us they're going to go see a movie...and spend another night at a hotel. After I close the door, I feel that nervousness again.

"Do you want more coffee or anything? Cake?" I ramble.

He shakes his head. "Larry and Peter seem to like each other a lot."

"Yeah, they do. I have to admit I wasn't sure how you were going to react to Peter being gay," I tell him. "I mean I know I told you last year, but we didn't really talk much." I blush thinking about that make out session under the tree.

He grins at me and then says, "I'm not really surprised, about Peter. Were you?"

"Yeah..."

"How'd he tell you?"

How do I tell this story? "It's long story."

"I'm not going anywhere."

I try to stop feeling shaky. "Let's sit in the living room. I'm gonna make some chamomile tea." To calm the f- down!

I make the tea for both of us, and we sit on the couch.

"So, what happened?"

"We were hanging out at his house and he made this dinner, but I guess I wasn't feeling well because I threw up all over the table after the first bite." I omit that I was in a deep depression because of the deadness that was my life. Spending hours editing the literary magazine and banging out weepy poems about...him.

"Then Peter gets me cleaned up... and my clothes are covered in throw-up so he took them off and put me in the shower."

"Now why didn't that ever happen when I was around?"

"I'm sure it would have if you ever cooked me dinner."

"Very funny. Continue." Justin leans back into the couch and smiles the sexiest smile ever. "So, you're naked and Peter is washing your naked body. So far I really like this story."

"Afterwards he put me in this robe and brought me to his room."

"Sounds romantic."

"It would have been if..."

"Peter wasn't gay."

"Right. But we aren't there yet. I'm on his bed and so is he. He's rubbing my feet."

"Are you positive Peter is gay?"

"When I tell you the next part, you'll see. So, something comes over me." I check Justin's expression. He's dying to hear this. "I lean forward, and I guess my boob falls out, and I see that it's kind of there and I lean into Peter and put my boob in his hand."

Justin is leaning forward with his eyes wide now and I'm kind of sideways on the couch.

"God, that is hot." We both laugh. "What happened?"

"Nothing. Not a squeeze. It was like he was holding my elbow or something."

The visual in Justin's mind...

"Nothing."

"Nothing."

"Shit," he shakes his head. "He's definitely gay. Then what?"

"I look over at the Tom Cruise poster on his wall." I shake my head. "That's when it hits me. And I say it, 'You're gay.'"

"And that was it."

"Sort of ...Peter had this whole secret relationship with this guy on the football team and the guy turned psycho and threatened to kick the shit out of him if he told anyone."

"Peter? Secret relationship?"

"I know! It gets better. He actually wrote this anonymous letter to the school paper editor, which was me. Susan and I spent all this time trying to figure out who anonymous was, but it was actually Peter, and it turned into this huge thing at school. The three of us actually wrote this article about bullying and homophobia. It won this national anti-bullying award. Then we went to Washington..." For a moment, I am transcended to that time period, as depressed as I was, that was a cool moment.

"Was that all before he came out to you?"

"It was all at the same time. It was crazy." I sigh and lean back into the couch so that now we are shoulder to shoulder.

We sit and say nothing. I can hear the peepers outside. The breeze comes through the open window in front of us. My heart pounds and pounds. And then...

He takes my hand and runs his fingers over mine and involuntarily my knee pushes into his.

"Do you remember what I said to you last year?"

Movie moment.

"I would wait for us."

God, I love his eyes, so soft like a gray kitten with fur so new it looks blue and his mouth so perfect too.

"I had a kind of shitty few years. When I saw you, I had just started to smoke and drink a lot...again. It was minor—it didn't last long—but it kind of sent me backwards a little, and I didn't call you or try to contact you until later, when my shit was together again."

I squeeze his hand. It all makes sense.

"You know I haven't really had a girlfriend...nothing that lasted. I mean, it didn't help that most of my interaction with girls was when we had these dances, and you know what...if you lock a bunch of girls up at a boarding school and then let them out only once in a while to see boys, they can be kind of slutty." He runs his free hand over his hair. I am jealous of that other hand. "Not to mention that none of those girls could match up to you."

That's all it takes for me to put my hand on his face and kiss him. He pulls away and traces my lips with his finger and then kisses me back. His tongue slides over my lips like his fingers did. "I've wanted to kiss you since I saw you at the restaurant when you first got to California. But I wanted to wait. With you grandmother and everything it seemed, I don't know. Not the right time."

I nod. "It's the right time now." Now we kiss the way I imagined we would. A kind of kiss that signified how much time had passed and how much we've changed and grown.

· · · · ·

I open my eyes. Sunlight blinds me. I roll over. Justin. His eyes peacefully closed and the lashes sweeping against his skin. The tiny patch of hair on his chest and the curve of the muscles on his arms. I reach over and touch him. Yep. This is real.

After we kissed on the couch and talked for a while, Justin brought me upstairs (with Peter and Larry gone, I took my room back) to "tuck me in" because Tony made him promise to come home by 1 am.

When we got to my room I didn't flip the overhead light on. Just the lamp on the side of my bed. In the semi-darkness I turned to Justin and said innocently, "I have to put on my PJ's."

He broke into a grin. "Can I help?"

I turned back around, shy and nervous and lifted my shirt over my head. When I reached around to unhook my bra, my hand touched his. "Let me help," he whispered.

I don't want to move to leave the bed, but my breath is horribly tainted by the morning. It would be nice to smell good when he wakes up. I roll to the other side to get up but feel a grip on my arm.

"No." He rubs my arm. "No leaving."

"But I want to brush my teeth."

"No."

"But I have to go to the bathroom."

"No."

"Justin!"

He opens his eyes. Hello ocean on a rainy day...hello perfect man for me...

He bats them at me. I laugh. "You think that will do it?"

"Yup!"

I turn to get up again, and this time he rolls on top of me and pins me down.

I look down and see his boxers have SpongeBob on them. Did I not notice this last night. I burst out laughing.

"You thought they were hot last night."

"It was dark."

"It was. But not too dark for me to remember the color of your panties."

"Don't cheat!" I snatch the covers down, so he can't peak.

"Pink and white polka dots."

"Wrong!"

"Let me check." He slides down, but I stop him.

"I'm sorry but as much as I like you, I am not fooling around until I brush my teeth and hoping you will do the same."

He rolls off me and puts his arms behind his head. "I'm glad I tucked you in last night."

I pull on my t-shirt and grin at him. "Me, too."

We walk to the bathroom leaning into each other and he tickles me, and I swat at him. We share my toothbrush, grinning and bumping each other.

I wipe my mouth on the towel and turn to Justin and he pulls me to him and we kiss. We kind of kiss and fumble our way back to the bedroom and tumble onto the bed. Last night we made out and touched each other, but nothing really serious.

But now it's all feeling very, *very* possible that things may happen, and I really feel like it's Disclaimer Time.

I stop kissing him. "Wait." Although he isn't doing anything.

"Huh?" He mumbles into my neck.

"I'm a virgin." It's a declarative, with the hint of an inquiry.

He stops kissing me and absolutely nothing can be heard for a full thirty seconds. Then he laughs.

I push him off me and sit all the way up. "It's funny?"

"No?"

I punch his arm. "Stop! I'm being serious. I'm just, you know, letting you know in case you didn't. Know."

"I kind of figured by the way you talked about Zak and Sean that you haven't—Oh, I see. You think—" he gestures to the rumbled sheets.

The blushing is so apparent, I can see it on my arms, for god's sake. "No, I mean..."

"Of course, yes I want you and I want to. But, I mean, it's our first date technically and I—" He makes his face in this mock choir boy (Jewish choir boy) kind of expression. "I am not that kind of boy."

I burst out laughing. Then I say, "Are you?"

"What?"

"Are you a virgin?"

He scratches his head. "Here's the thing. Uh, did you ever, have you ever...did you and Sean? Wait, not an image I want to picture. But did you ever *almost* do it or *kind of* do it?"

"Isn't that like being *sort of* pregnant or something? I don't think there's like a gray area."

"One time, I half way did it. You know, like just the tip."

Which just kind of hangs in the air, the word tip. Visual and everything. I shake my head. "Oh! I think I know what you mean. But, no. That's never happened to me."

Now the conversation completely stops, and nothing moves and then we both burst out laughing.

"Your question was, have I had sex before? And the answer, Maddie, is...no. Not totally and fully and completely, so that's a no." His face is red now. "And I don't have condoms, and as neurotic as you think you are, I'm probably twice. Not interested in being a baby daddy right now. Gotta finish high school, you know?"

Different topic. I take it. "What do you mean?"

"I have to go back and finish school. I didn't go in as a junior. Prep schools make you repeat the previous year if you start after freshmen year."

His school is in Massachusetts's near Emerson and not far from Connecticut. I grab a pillow and lean back into the headboard.

Justin scoots next to me. "By the way, with all this going on, I haven't even asked what's up with you. What are you doing in September?" He moves the hair off my shoulders and touches my skin.

Ugh. Thought I could completely tuck away the last nine months of my life before California.

I can't look at him, so I stare at my hands that clutch the pillow. "I had a kind of melt down at the beginning of the school year and the long and short is that I am not going to college—Emerson—until January." Justin shifts but says nothing, and I still don't look at him. "Now I don't know what to do. I was going to try and get a part time job here. I was going to take a writing class at Berkley but now everything seems so uncertain, and I guess that whole 'life happens when you're making plans' thing is true."

He takes my hand and then pulls me close. Then he says out loud what I was thinking: "Emerson is not far from where I'll be." He kisses my fingertips, and we hold each other for a while and for the first time in I don't know how long, I stop worrying.

·   ·   ·   ·   ·

My phone buzzes just as I open my eyes and yawn. We must have fallen back asleep. I turn and reach for the phone. Peter.

"Seriously, can't you just walk up here?" I say when I answer.

Justin is awake now, too. Lying on his side and looking adorable. Blue eyes sleepy. Hair rumpled.

He leans in and says into the phone, "Yeah, we aren't naked or anything."

I punch his arm.

"Ow!" He rolls away for a second but then rolls back to me.

"I'm not downstairs," Peter says.

"Still at the hotel?" Justin sticks his tongue in my ear. I push him away but smile.

"Where are you?"

"At the airport."

"Airport?" Justin rolls back and his face falls to serious.

"Where's Larry?"

"Don't know." He sighs heavily. "My guess is that he left sometime around midnight."

Oh, *no.*

"You know what, it was fine. He was weird. He was definitely hiding something, Maddie. I should have known with that whole gay test bullshit."

I watch Justin sit up and stretch. It's way too beautifully distracting. "What happened?"

"We just got into this weird fight where he started saying that I had a problem with him being a Christian or something. I mean all I said to him was how can you be a Christian, when Christians tend to have problems with gays? He went off and 'they hate the sin not the sinner' and I just said *whoa* so being gay is a sin? He said some bullshit about 'No, only if you act on it' and I told him 'we've been acting on it' and he said some more bullshit about 'I know, but if we ask Jesus for forgiveness' and then I thought, oh, shit no way am not going back into the closet. Especially for Jesus." We laugh at that one.

"But how did you wind up at the airport?"

"We were sitting in the car in front of the condo when this all happened, didn't even make it to the hotel...me and break ups in cars...and I said 'You should just go, you should just drive back home, and he said the most messed up thing: 'You're right. This is all devil's work.' I just said, 'Have a nice life' and went inside. Man, I really can pick them. I couldn't sleep, so I called my mom, and she got me the ticket and here I am at a layover in Ohio."

Justin puts his hand on top of mine.

"I was going to stay, but I think you and Justin have this perfect opportunity to be together. And from watching you do the third wheel thing that is clearly not fun. So, I'm going home. Maybe I'll go for that internship my dad talked to me about."

No Bubbie. No Peter. Just us.

"Maddie?"

"No, I'm here. I'm going to miss you."

"Oh, and I should tell you something else."

"What?"

"There was no little brother who died of leukemia. He's an only child."

Of course, there was no brother. Isn't that an oxymoron—Christian liar?

Justin's thumb strokes the top of my hand. I close my eyes. "I'll really miss you, Peter."

"Me too. Tell Helen I'm thinking of her."

"I will." I squeeze Justin's hand and say goodbye.

CHAPTER ELEVEN
A CABIN IN THE WOODS

"You have some sauce—" Justin leans over and dabs my face with his napkin. "You're good." Then he takes a huge bite of his pizza.

I laugh. "Come here." Now I lean over and wipe his face.

"Enough kissy face, you two lovebirds." Tony walks over in his white apron and wipes his hands before putting them on Justin's shoulders. "You two should go take a few days and get out of here."

"You're actually giving me some time off?"

Tony squeezes Justin and he yelps. "Only if it's to be with the lovely Maddie who is nothing but a good influence on you." He winks at me then slaps Justin on the back, which causes him to almost choke. Then he lays a key down on the table. "Here's the key to the cabin up in Tahoe. I'll let you take the truck. Then he leans down and says into Justin's ear, "Pack a raincoat or two, *capiche*?"

Justin turns beet red and I laugh. A *raincoat*.

"Okay, kiddos. Time to make the pizza. Let me know when you are leaving, and listen, don't come back till Friday. *Capiche*?"

"*Capiche!*" we both say.

Almost a whole week alone...Hope it rains.

•   •   •   •   •

"That's sweet of Tony. And I'm sorry to hear about Peter. That's too bad. Larry seemed like a nice guy." Bubbie sounds good.

"We want to stop and visit you guys on the way back on Friday. Will that work?"

"Yes, of course."

"You really need to stay there two weeks?"

"I do, honey. I really do."

"Will Joyce stay with you?"

"No, she's going next Monday."

Silence.

"I just feel like I don't really understand what's going on."

"I know. You just have to trust me."

I think for a minute. "Did you talk to Mom again?"

"She told me her plan to come down and drag me back to chemo. Not a surprise." She laughs.

I don't laugh. "We're just scared, you know."

She stops laughing. "I know, and I appreciate all the love and concern. And I'm not stopping your mother from coming down. She said that she would give me two weeks. So, I expect her when I return home."

I just can't put any more energy into trying to convince her. I can feel it inside that she's pretty resolute. I wish I had my journal with me.

"Go have a beautiful week with your sweetheart. He really has grown into a lovely man."

I have to smile. "Thanks. I'll see you Friday."

. . . . . .

The cabin is straight out of a fairy tale, tucked into the woods. Just two bedrooms, a brick fire place, cushy furniture. A hammock in the front and a grille on a bamboo deck off the back.

I stand in the foyer of the cabin and survey it all. Justin opens all the windows up and recites some of the things we can do. "...and then take a walk around the lake and then swim, but I think we might need wet suits. It's still kind of cold..."

I'm all smiles, holding my backpack with my journal in the front pocket and my favorite pillow I can't sleep without.

Justin washes his hands in the kitchen sink, and wipes them on a towel, slowly, like he's thinking. He comes over and takes my bag and pillow. "You gotta see the master bedroom and the hot tub outside..."

The rest of the grand tour is brief and ends with us tumbling into the king size bed as soon as we finish putting fresh sheets on it. The sunlight pours into the room through the skylights and the ceiling fan creates the perfect breeze. These are things I think of when I look down and see that I've somehow removed all my clothes and he has done the same.

I lie on my back and stare at the ceiling fan's whirling. Justin whispers something in my ear but it's unclear. I don't really care what he's saying because I just want to feel this moment in a way that will stay with me— inked in permanent marker on my brain. I don't want it to fade like handwriting on old paper. I roll over so that I'm on top of him and run my hands over his chest. He reaches up and puts a hand on either side of my face and brings me down to him and whispers again in my ear. This time I hear him.

"I love you."

I remember other times that I heard those words. Zak. Sean. Neither time did I respond with anything other than changing the subject.

But this time I look right into Justin's eyes and say, "I love you, too."

•　　•　　•　　•　　•

The Good Feeling didn't stay with me though. Moments after losing my virginity, while Justin falls fast asleep, I slip out of bed and walk into the kitchen. My heart pounds and I feel sweaty. I gulp down a glass of water.

I haven't had a panic attack in months. I didn't even bring my Rescue Remedy with me to the cabin. I didn't bring any of the anti-anxiety meds to California at all.

Can't call Peter. Definitely can't bother Bubbie. Hell, I'd take talking to my mother right now.

Shit.

I look around the kitchen and then the living room for something. I don't even know what. I see a coffee table with some books on architecture and cooking. In the kitchen, I see way too many wooden spoons in a carafe and a ton of cutting boards piled up on the side of the fridge. A picture of

Tony and some woman is held with a magnet on the side of the fridge. But there's my backpack on the table with my journal sticking out.

I grab the bag then rummage around the kitchen and find a pen in a drawer full of knick-knacks. I plop on the comfy couch. Before I open the journal, I sit with my eyes closed and try to do some of this *ujjayi* breathing that I remember from all those yoga classes with Barbara. I don't know how much time passes, but my heart slows down. I pick up the pen.

I don't know what I'm feeling.

My breath was all choppy and my heart hurt.

But now my breath is smooth, and my thoughts are becoming more clear.

Maybe I'm just scared.

Was Peter right? Will I screw this all up?

What am I afraid of?

I don't know what's coming next. The first time in my life I don't know what's next, and I don't know what to do or what I want— No, I'm just afraid of what I want and if I give into it, I might lose again. I just don't want to lose anyone again.

.   .   .   .   .

I close the notebook with the pen in it and sit with my breath and body just pulsing and beating. I hear the faint sound of the fan whirling in the bedroom and a kind of hooting outside. I walk to the bay window and look out into the darkness and just see the shadows of all the tall trees. I open a side window and just breathe in the air. It's kind of sharp and smells of the lake and dirt. All I want is to calm down, calm down so I don't bolt, which is what I want to do. I can see myself taking the keys that hang on the key hook by the door, and darting out into the darkness, barefoot and barely dressed, backpack over my shoulder. I see myself turning on the car and driving...driving back to Connecticut and forgetting Justin and Bubbie and everything. But I think of a Bubbism that's like an old country song, better to have lost at love then never to have loved at all. I grab my notebook and sit down again.

CHAPTER TWELVE
"DO YOU NEED A DOCTOR?"

"Maddie?" I feel myself being nudged in the shoulder. I'm on my stomach and turn my head and open my eyes.

Justin's face, eyebrows knitted together, looms in front of mine. "Holy shit. You scared me when I reached over to hug you this morning and all I got was an armful of pillows. My uncle has a shitload of pillows."

I bury my head into my arms and groan.

"Are you okay?" He strokes my back. "Does it...hurt?"

"A little," I say into my arms.

"Can you walk?"

Turning all the way so he can see my face, I say with complete seriousness, "Barely."

"Oh man! Do you need a doctor or something?" He looks worried.

I burst out laughing.

"Very funny." He nudges me again but then kisses the top of my head.

I sit up and he sits next to me. "That was a big deal to me, last night. I just want you to know that."

I nod. But he looks at me like he's waiting for me to say something else.

"And what we said to each other, you know," he looks nervous. "What we said. It means something. It means a lot."

I stand up and go to the kitchen. "Are you hungry? I'm starving." I open the fridge. "We have a bottle of water and a couple sticks of butter. Yum." I keep opening and closing cabinets.

Justin walks into the kitchen. "What are you doing?"

I hold up a box of Bisquick from the cabinet. "Maybe making pancakes?"

He snatches it from me and says, "You need milk and eggs."

"Right."

He waits a beat and then says, "Maddie, do you want to be with me?"

I turn back to the cabinet pretending to look for more ingredients.

My heart is pounding so hard. I have to just turn around and say it or the anticipation will give me a heart attack.

I close the cabinet and without turning say to the counter top. "I'm just scared."

He's behind me, arms circling my waist. "Me, too."

We just stand there for a minute. Then I say, "Okay."

"Don't sound so excited."

I turn around and kiss him on the mouth.

"That's better," he says.

·   ·   ·   ·   ·

I give in and forget the outside world for the rest of the week but on Thursday afternoon as we are packing to leave early Friday morning, I feel the familiar burning behind my ears and twitch in my eye. The anxiety monster returns. By now, I've spilled the entire story about my mental melt down to Justin so he's on to me before I can head for the hills screaming.

I'm frantically scrubbing the kitchen countertop and have just spent the last hour scrubbing every single cleared off surface in the house when Justin comes up behind me and says the only thing that stops me:

"Your mom called. She wants her sponge back."

I stop mid-scrub and glare at him.

"Easy now, just put down the sponge, carefully *carefully*!"

I throw the sponge into the sink and cross my arms.

Justin puts his arms around me, but I don't budge.

"You're freaking out." He says into the top of my head. Then he puts his chin there and says, "But I'm trying to figure out if it's because of me or your grandmother."

I turn around and put my arms around his waist and say into his chest, "Both."

"What are you so worried about with us?"

"The end."

"What end?"

"The inevitable end of us...again."

"Why do we have to end?"

I don't have an answer but that need-to-know list pops into my head. The only good thing to come from Larry. I never even began that list and suddenly there are things that I *need to know*.

"Do you still have the picture my sister painted of you?"

He breaks into a grin. "Yes. It's hanging in my room in Florida. The only thing that hangs in my room. What does that have to do with—"

"Have you watched *The Princess Bride* in the last few years?"

His smile turns to serious. "Yes," he says quietly.

"And did you ever think of me when it came on?"

"Yes, every time, and I would only change it if one of my friends came into my room 'cause you know guys don't exactly watch *The Princess Bride*."

I'm cataloging his answers into the drawers of my mind, but I keep firing away at these things on my list. They are like a stack of index cards filled with questions. "What do you do to make sure you don't drink or smoke pot?"

His face clouds for a minute. "I just don't do it. Sometimes I go to meetings if I'm feeling fucked up."

"And how do you plan on us staying together after we both leave California?"

"I'll drive to Emerson every weekend, and you'll come up to see me."

"What about my parents?"

"I'll win them over with my charm."

"You have an answer for everything."

He reaches out and pulls me close to him. "No, I don't. I just know what I want."

We hold each other in the silence, save for this one damn bird that's been chirping an afternoon revelry every day we've been here.

"Can't that bird shut up," I say, finally.

"I don't hear anything," he whispers.

· · · · ·

"But why hasn't she called me the entire week? Why didn't she or Joyce return my voicemails?"

Justin pops the GPS back into the holder and grabs his sunglasses from the center console. "I don't know, but I do think if something was wrong, they would call you."

Which happens just as we are about to get into the car. My cell phone buzzes, and I know, like you just know these types of things, before I answer it that it's Joyce.

"Maddie," I hear her sigh and I don't want to hear the next set of sentences that are about to come out of her mouth. "Helen was admitted this morning."

"What happened?" I shut my eyes.

"I'm not sure. She went to the bathroom last night, and she was in there a while and they knocked on the door and when she didn't answer, they opened the door, and she was passed out on the floor and there was all this blood..."

"Oh, God."

"But the good news is that she is in the hospital right now and she's resting. I'm sorry I didn't call sooner. They are prepping her for a colonoscopy right now. The plan is to do it in the morning."

"What do they think is happening?"

"No one wants to say exactly, but I did manage to get the doctor to speak frankly with me and he said that she probably has some more tumors." She pauses, and I let that kind of go down into my body. "I called your parents a few minutes ago, and they are getting on the next plane."

"Should we head out to you guys?"

"Come in the morning."

"Okay." I say because there's nothing else I can do.

When I hang up the phone, I say to Justin, "Not good,"

"Do you want to leave now?"

"I don't know."

He puts his arm around me. "Whatever you want to do, Maddie, I'm here."

"I know, "I say. "I know."

CHAPTER THIRTEEN
MOM

The steamy air in the recovery room makes my whole body sweat. Justin and I hold clammy hands and sit on the couch in front of the hospital bed where Bubbie lies, her head uncovered, signs of her gray hair coming back in and a half smile splayed across her face.

I lean in to Justin and whisper, "Thank God that noise finally stopped."

BEEP...BEEP... BEEP...

"Oh, God. Not again." I close my eyes and try to collect the burning anger inside.

BEEP...BEEP... BEEP...

"What the hell!" *BEEP...* "Doesn't anyone else hear this friggin' beeping?" My voice is an octave from a yell. I glance over at Bubbie, but she doesn't even twitch. Those drugs are that good.

BEEP... BEEP... BEEP...

"That's it!" I throw both hands up in the air.

BEEP... BEEP... BEEP...

Justin grabs my hands and puts them both in his lap. He looks at me and says, "You have to calm down. The machine is broken. Remember that's what they said and they're coming back with a new one—"

The blue of Justin's eyes does the trick for a moment. I nod, try to take a deep breath, but the friggin' *BEEP... BEEP... BEEP* causes me to start coughing on the inhale. Justin whacks me on the back, and Joyce rushes over with water. "I'm fine!" I bark at both of them. Joyce leaves the water on the coffee table in front of the couch and scurries away. Justin holds the cup in front of me. I sulk but take a sip.

That's when Bubbie opens her eyes and says softly, "Thirsty."

I leap up from the couch, but Joyce, already holding a cup of water, beats me.

Magically the beeping stops.

"Here," Joyce leans down and brings it to Bubbie's mouth, holding it while she sips. I slide my hand over Bubbie's. It's warm and soft.

After just a moment, Bubbie pushes the cup away and Joyce puts it back on the table, then busies herself with organizing the water pitcher, cups, and packages of saltines.

Bubbie squeezes my hand firmly, smiles, and then her eyes fall closed. Back to dreamland.

Joyce is right next to me immediately. Again. "Saltine?" she asks.

I shake my head.

"I'll take one," Justin says to her from the couch. She grabs enough to feed the entire hospital floor and dumps them on his lap.

"Whoa! Uh, thanks." He gives me a silly smile and mouths, "I'm not even hungry." I start to relax and then—

BEEP... BEEP... BEEP...

"Oh, come on!"

Joyce waves me off and straightens a pillow on the couch...even though Justin had been using it to lean on. He almost falls over.

"You shouldn't worry." She says pounding the pillow into submission. Justin scoots closer to the end of the couch, saltines in tow. She continues, "They've been coming in here and checking her pulse by hand."

"But the sound is driving me crazy!" I explode and stomp out of the room. I fly down to the nurses' station, grab the first nurse, and say, "Please make that stupid beeping stop!" Without a flinch or change of expression she says, "Just a minute."

I watch her disappear behind the circular desk. All my fatigue just hits me, and I slump into a plastic chair next to the wall. No one will tell me what's happening. If Bubbie is okay. Where are my parents? They should be here. If Mom were here she'd have this all figured out. I straighten up. "I just have to channel a little Mom," I say to the nurse who looks at me like I've landed on the last spaceship from Pluto.

•   •   •   •   •

When I return to the room, the noise is gone. In the silence of Bubbie's breathing, Joyce knits. Justin watches a muted episode of *How I Met Your Mother* without laughing.

I sit next to him. He squeezes my knee but stays engrossed in the show. Joyce glances up at us from the rocking chair next to the head of the bed. Now she's calmed down to the point of knitting. The fuchsia knitting needles dance between her fingers, reflecting the harsh hospital light, bouncing pink flashes across the dreary walls. I sigh and lay my head on Justin's knee. A tiny hero scar is still there. Fourth grade. Wrestling this punk who called us a bunch of Jew-Jew bees, to the ground. Wonder if that kid's nose ever recovered from Justin's fist? I trace the scar with my finger. And I breathe in. Deeply.

"When is the doctor coming in with the results, Joyce?" I say, sitting up on the sticky hospital couch. Sweat beads above my lip. Justin, who seems unaffected by the temperature in this room moves with me, still holding me.

Joyce pauses mid stitch and glances up at the clock above the TV. "He said he'd be around four."

"Fifteen minutes," I say.

"Another round of *How I Met Your Mother*?" Justin says.

•   •   •   •   •

"Helen's cancer has spread."

Dr. Nelson is young, so young I almost don't believe a word he says. But his voice is even and doctorly.

Justin has gone to retrieve us coffee. Joyce sits next to me across from Dr. Nelson. We are in his office, which is taken up mainly by the enormous mahogany desk and two chairs for—I guess—family members or patients. How many other people has he told that they or their grandmother, wife, or son has cancer? How many times has he said, "You're cancer free!"

"What's the next step?" My mother's voice comes out of me now. This is what she would do. Not get hysterical. Get the action plan.

"I would like to keep her here over night. Tomorrow I want to begin radiation and chemotherapy." He stops and picks up a piece of paper. "I called over to her surgeon at County and they said she was doing chemo but had stopped?"

"Yes, we were over at the holistic center."

"Yes, you told me that," he sounds irritated. "But I assumed that she was done with her treatments?"

"No," Joyce gazes down at her lap. I touch her shoulder. She lets out a sob.

The doctor looks at me. "I want to be very clear with you both. With the treatment, her chances are fair to good."

"And without?" I ask.

He doesn't say anything.

"We can't do anything without Helen making the decision." Joyce dabs her eyes with a tissue and directs this to the doctor.

I try not to leap up and strangle her. Then a knock at the door.

"Dr. Nelson?"

Mom! Impeccable timing as usual.

CHAPTER FOURTEEN
TIGHT GRIP

But nothing happens because all my mother says, after reaching down to quickly hug me and cast a quick unsmiling glance at Joyce, is, "Where's Mom?" Her face is tired, with only a sheen of lip-gloss and the faint traces of blush.

Dr. Nelson looks surprised, and he gestures to the only empty seat on the other side of me next to the desk. "Let's talk a minute Mrs.—"

"Call me Bernice, doctor," she says smoothing her hair. "This is my husband, Stanley." Dad smiles at me and I give a little wave.

Dr. Nelson nods. "Please take a seat, Bernice. I can get another chair."

But my father shakes his head. Then he says with great professor authority, "We would like to see Helen, if you don't mind."

"How about if we talk a bit first?"

My mother frowns at the doctor. "The nurse directed me to see you, Dr. Nelson but I would like to see my mother first. I'm sure you understand. We can talk after."

I guess Dr. Nelson knows how to deal with a resolute woman because he sighs and says, "That would be fine. Let me get the nurse to escort you all back and then we can have a chat."

"Thank you." My mother grabs my hand in one of hers and my father's in the other. "Let's go." When Joyce stands up to follow, Mom's blue eyes are steal. "We can take it from here, Joyce."

Joyce surprises me. "I understand. I left my cell number with the nurses. Could you give me a call later in the day and update me?"

"Of course," my mom says and then ushers us all out the door.

．　　．　　．　　．　　．

Mom leads us out of the office and down the hallway. As we pass the nurses' station where a nurse holds a hand up and calls for us to wait a moment but then there's a ding from the elevator and out comes Justin with a tray of coffees.

My mother is so concentrated on her mission that she doesn't notice him, and her grip is so tight I can't stop walking either. I just look at him hopelessly, but he nods and follows behind.

"This is the room," I tell my mother, so she'll slow down. "She might still be sleeping."

But when we walk in, I smell the peanut butter first and instantly know she's awake.

"Hi!" She says waving a plastic knife with a smear of peanut butter on it. "I'm starving. You guys hungry?"

I let go of my mother's hand, but she grips it and moves us both to the side of the bed. "Hi," she says slowly. "Are you supposed to be eating?"

"Oh yeah! Aside from being a little out of it, I'm fine. There's plenty to share. Maddie, Justin. You kids hungry?" She smears the peanut butter on the cracker and then pops it in her mouth.

Finally, my mother turns around and sees Justin. Her face doesn't change. He smiles at her and still she does nothing. My father, in the meantime, has already said hello and is drinking one of the coffees.

"You remember Justin, honey?" My father slurps some coffee.

"Yes." She eyeballs him but not for long. She turns back to my grandmother. "Mom, I'm glad you are feeling better. We need to talk about all this, you know. They found tumors."

My grandmother reaches for another cracker. "Maddie, can you pour me some water? This peanut butter is damn sticky."

"Mom—"

My mother has let go of the death grip. I reach behind me for the cart with the pitcher of water, but Justin has already poured it and passes me the cup. Our fingers brush and my chest flutters. "I'm so glad she's here," I mouth. He nods and puts the pitcher down.

"Mom—"

"Thank you, Maddie," Bubbie says when I give her the water.

"Mom—"

Bubbie takes her time sipping the water. She closes her eyes and smiles, "Thirsty!"

"Mother!"

Now Bubbie looks at her and the tension in the room is thick. Not even one of mom's favorite slicing knives could cut it.

"Bernice." The lightness in Bubbie's face fades. "Bernice. I do not want to discuss this with you. I will have a chat with Dr. Nelson when he makes his rounds and then let you know what I decide."

"You're open to chemo?"

"No." Bubbie drinks the rest of the water. "More, please." She smiles brightly.

This is getting nuts. I snatch the cup. Bubbie frowns. "Listen, girls, I'm a grown up, and I'm going to deal with my cancer, yes, *my* cancer the way I want to."

"Just like the way you dealt with your drinking, the first, I don't know, ten times? Your way, really? And how did that go, Mother? Really, how did doing things your way go?"

The silence that follows so quiet I hear the very faint light rock music from the nurse's station down the hallway.

Now Bubbie's eyes fill with tears.

"Bern," My father reaches over and touches her shoulder. "Maybe that's enough."

My mother flinches and pushes Dad off her. "No. It's not enough." She grits her teeth and leans down so she is closer to Bubbie. "Listen to me, Mother I've almost lost you so many times to your way of doing things. I finally forced you to go to rehab, and I will do the same thing with chemo, so help me. Because I will not—" she stops and puts a finger to her lips and swallows. "I will not let you die, Mother. No way."

The bits and pieces of their relationship decades ago fall like shreds of paper around us, and then because this is the way life works, the stupid blood pressure machine begins to beep.

. . . . .

After the nurses rush in and check to make sure Bubbie still has a pulse, they push buttons and pull wires, trying to shut the machine off. Meantime the nurse's assistant comes in to change the bed linen, and Bubbie excuses herself to take a shower. We all file out of the room and go back to the main lounge. Dad tosses his empty coffee cup into a trashcan. We all sit side by side on the long couch. Justin still holds the other three in the paper tray. Mom reaches for one of them, Justin helps her loosen it, and she pops the cover off and takes a long drink. She even wipes her mouth after with the back of her hand.

Finally, she crosses her legs and turns to face him. "So, Justin, what have you been up to?"

Justin looks from me to my mother and back to me and then he tells her how life's been for the last two years. Dad, by now, although he's just downed a large coffee, leans back into the one cushiony chair in the lounge, and closes his eyes. I grab the last four sugar packets in the tray and open up the last coffee. Time to drink.

. . . . .

When Bubbie finishes her shower, the nurse comes to get us. When we walk in, Bubbie's soft gray hair is damp and her face has a nice pink to it.

"I just finished speaking to Dr. Nelson."

We all sit around the bed in the chairs and couch.

"I'm going home tomorrow," She tells us, then adds, "I called Joyce. She's picking me up." Her tone is not angry. It's even, normal.

I shake my head. I hear Justin kind of let out a sigh. My father shifts in his chair. I don't hear a thing from Mom.

"Bernice, I'd like you to stay for a few days. Spend some time together, but not time wasted on talking about my cancer. Barb is coming tonight, too."

"What about chemo?"

"I'm not doing it," Bubbie says quietly.

"Why?" I ask.

"Because it's poison. Because maybe I'm tired of fighting. Because I want to handle my cancer a certain way that mainstream medicine won't."

"And if you have another episode?" This is from my mom.

"I'll deal with it, if or when I have to."

My mother sighs and looks over at my father who says, "We'd love to stay a few more days, Helen."

My mother shakes her head. I reach for her hand, and she squeezes mine hard.

CHAPTER FIFTEEN
ANGEL

"Here, let me take something." I reach out and take a paper bag steaming with freshly baked bread.

"Thanks, angel." Tony kisses my cheek, leaving a fresh mark of garlic breath.

"Hey, Uncle Tony," Justin reaches around from behind me, and they grab hands and smack backs.

"Take this, my nephew." Tony gives him three large pizza boxes stacked on top of each other. "I have cannolis and *pizzafriet* in the car, too."

"Good afternoon," Tony and my mom kiss cheeks, and he and Dad do the same back slapping routine, Dad kind of fumbling his way through it, but they laugh.

Justin grabs my arm as he slides through the kitchen and back out to Tony's car. My mother busies herself with arranging the food on the table. My dad and Tony fly around the kitchen getting glasses and dishes, continuing a conversation from yesterday at breakfast (Tony and Justin came by yesterday before the restaurant opened) about fly-fishing, which they both did as kids.

I make my way through the hustle of the kitchen and glance out the back door to Barb, her cell phone to her ear, smiling and walking slowly back and forth. She's been on her phone with Cliff most of the hour she's been here.

Barb must see me out of the corner of her eye because she stops and looks up. "Everything okay?" She mouths to me. I nod.

Then before I even see her, I can smell her Chanel No. 5 perfume waft from behind. Then she whispers so only I can hear: "Does your sister have to be on the phone right now?"

Because Mom's had as much Al-Anon as me, she hasn't said a word this whole time to Barb but because no one can be by the Big Book all the time, Mom still has to say something to me. But I just shrug and push past her to go back to the kitchen.

Justin stands in the middle of the kitchen with an armload of more food in aluminum containers and paper bags. Mom comes back in and together we help him find a spot for everything. We can't manage it all on the table. Mom takes some and arranges it perfectly on the buffet against the back wall of the dining area in the kitchen.

Barb rejoins us, smiling, gives Justin and Tony a hug. I pull a chair out and sit next to Tony. I pour myself some Dr. Pepper. Every day this week has felt like a party.

When Bub finally emerges, oddly her hair seems to be growing in daily, now it looks like an intentional crew cut. She comes in yawning loudly and rubbing her eyes.

Tony stands up immediately and wipes his mouth before rushing to pull her chair out at the table. We all stop eating, and it gets quiet.

She sits down, her eyes half-mast. I feel a collective holding of breath among us. Some of the mornings (or afternoons) seem worse than others. Tony takes her hands in his and says softly, "You hungry?"

Her eyes open and she breaks into a grin. "Did you bring the *pizzafriet*?"

Relief across everyone's faces.

"Yes," Tony kisses each hand. "Yes, I did."

· · · · ·

Three weeks pass in a similar fashion, minus my parents, who return home. Bubbie, miraculously, changes her mind about chemo. I think it was the second conversation with Tony on the back porch when she came home that did it. What it was, she won't discuss it. She commits to one month. Then, she says she will reevaluate. She also only agrees to chemo three days a week, sleeping 12 to 24 hours a day on off days after and managing to be up and around on the weekends. She's not smoking the marijuana but taking it in pill form. It helps considerably with her appetite, especially when Tony brings *pizzafriet,* which has turned into every day. The worst part of chemo now is simply that she's wiped out and has really dry skin. The best part for both of us is Tony and Justin.

One night she says to me, as I help her apply some cocoa butter on her arms and legs, which have taken the worse of the chemo beating, "Who would have ever thought that my normal would involve being waited on by a burly Italian man."

To which I reply, "Who would have thought my normal would involve my ex-boyfriend and watching his uncle fall for my Bubbie?"

"Oh, stop that!" But her checks flush.

"He is falling for you." I kneel in front of her as she sits on the bed and roll up her overalls. She has lost a lot of weight despite all the food from Tony. Her legs seem so thin. "I don't care how nice a person is, no guy, especially a macho man like Tony would sit with you while you watch those sappy old movies like *Bridges of Madison County*...and with you asleep half the time. On his shoulder, might I add."

She smiles somewhere between shy and happy.

I close up the cream and kiss her goodnight and thank God for another day.

.　　.　　.　　.　　.

A few days later, in the morning while Bubbie is still sleeping, I scribble a note and leave it on the table on the off chance she wakes up before ten. Then I take off for a run. It's the first time in a long time, and so I run pretty far, until I reach Fisherman's wharf, which is a good five miles away, if you cut through some back roads. The salty damp air cool, and my skin pricking with goose bumps from the sweat cooling on my skin. I stop running when I get to the wharf where Justin and I had our first day together in San Francisco. I lean over the rail on the dock and catch my breath. I look at the ocean flat and calm, bluer than the ocean at home.

Instinctively I reach for my cell phone clipped to my waist. No calls. All is well. I reach into my bra and take out the four bucks I brought for a cup of tea at my favorite tea place. Wow, this is the first time I've been alone in a few weeks. I walk down the dock, the sound of seagulls calling.

I can't remember ever being this happy in my life.

Reggae music plays while I sit outside the Tea House drinking some cinnamon apple tea. A guy wearing short shorts bikes by on a unicycle like it's normal. A mom and her toddler sit at the other table diagonal from me. The toddler stares at me while drinking chocolate milk through a straw. Her mother talks seriously into her cell phone. I sip the tea out of the paper cup and think about my coffee shop at home, my over sugared lattes. I could get used to cinnamon apple tea in the morning just like I have gotten used to Justin every day. I take another drink of tea, smile at the little girl still staring at me.

I toss the cup in the garbage next to my table and stand up and stretch, inhaling the perfect smells of the coffee shop and the ocean.

"Maddie!"

I stop stretching. "Tony, hey. I was just gonna run down to the restaurant."

I stop talking because the look on his face. My insides kind of cave in.

"What happened?" I ask.

He takes my arm and pulls me close. I can't hear what he's saying but I feel a little bit of a *déjà vu* or time warp or something. It's the same kind of summer day but hot, and I'm at camp and we've just pulled into the parking lot. Zak and his parents never showed up at dinner, so we drove back and when we get out of the car, my friend Beth running towards me, crying and red, she was so red. That's what I remember and then...Me saying something. I think it was—

"No!" Which is what I say right now.

Tony is crying. "We spent the night together...I snuck in through the window." He smiles as the tears roll. "We didn't want to tell you. And this morning...she didn't wake up."

What? I just left the house? How?

He's fully crying, choking. "We held each other." He shakes his head. "All—all night." Now he completely crumbles, holds himself up with one of the chairs at a table in the front of the restaurant. "I woke up...and put my hand on her shoulder, and she was so cold. I called 911 and screamed for you, angel. I called Justin and then I saw the note you left."

"Where's Justin?"

"At the—"

But he doesn't finish his sentence.

I put a hand on his heaving shoulder. Then I feel my own body give out, and I sink into the chair next to him and we hold each other and cry.

CHAPTER SIXTEEN
EULOGY

Birds circle us overhead and the ocean laps. Rabbi Andrew's prayer shawl blows in the wind, and he puts a hand on his yarmulke to keep it from flying off. "Please rise as we say the Mourner's Kaddish."

My legs are steel posts when I stand.

The Rabbi begins, *"Yit'gadal v'yit'kadash sh'mei raba."* Under the tent, a chorus of "Amens" follow.

As the Rabbi continues in Hebrew, I glance at Tony. He's mouthing the words like he's done this before. *"B'al'ma di v'ra khir'utei v'yam'likh mal'khutei b'chayeikhon uv'yomeikhon."*

Even though I don't know what each Hebrew word means, the sounds coming from us as we stand together on the beach saying goodbye to Bubbie feel like tiny pins pricking the back of my head.

My eyes fall on the solid brass urn on a table next to the Rabbi, surrounded by bouquets of brightly colored flowers. I scan the crowd of about sixty. Reds, purples, blues. No one is wearing black.

"I'd like to call up Helen's granddaughter, Maddie."

Standing up takes a long time for me. People murmur. Justin looks worried. My parents pat my legs. When I finally stand and begin to make my way, I want to stop moving. Each step is weighted with my not wanting to be in this moment. I'm surprised when I reach the Rabbi and feel his warm hand on my shoulder. I turn to the crowd of sad and silent faces.

I don't have anything prepared, so when I open my mouth I expect to just cry. Instead I talk:

"I tried to write something for today and when that didn't work, I tried to go through Bubbie's journals for one of her poems. But truthfully, I hurt too much. It hurts to stand here. It hurts to tell you all how much I miss her, how much I don't want to be here before all of you, how much I don't want to do this. It hurts to turn the pages of her journals. To read her handwriting. To sit in her favorite chair in her bedroom. Everything, every part of me hurts...But I take some comfort in knowing that I'm not alone in my pain. In my hurt about losing my grandmother too soon, way too soon. Just this morning before we left the house, I tried one last attempt to come up with the proper eulogy for Bubbie and that's when I remembered something she said to me not too long ago when I told her how she had to try everything to stay alive because I didn't want to go through this." I wave my arms around the room. "And she came back at me with one of her Bubbiesm except this one came from one of her favorite writers E.B. White, 'Never worry about your heart till it stops beating.' And then she added, as long as you are alive and beating, sweetie, things will hurt." I stop and look at the faces of my mother, father, sister, Justin, and Tony and I add, "And I hurt," I laugh while the tears fall, "so I guess I don't have to worry."

.   .   .   .   .

I come forward and take the urn out of the Rabbi's hands. I hear my mother sob and my father reassure her. Then we all file out of the tent. The only sound is the ocean moving. We walk down to the water, all together, Justin holds my hand and my parents are on the right of me with Barbara and Cliff and Peter. Joyce nods her head at me. I slide out of my shoes and step into the water. I gasp from how cool it is on my feet, and then I open the urn, let go of Justin's hand, step a little in the water and scatter the ashes.

.   .   .   .   .

My hands slide around the stack of my grandmother's notebooks, and I place them gently in the box. I close the flaps and keep my fingers pressed on the opening. Justin pulls out a piece of packing tape and lays it across the flaps. We don't talk. The only sound the hum of the ceiling fan in my grandmother's bedroom and the far away sound of the ocean through the open windows.

It's the last box. Justin takes my hand and says, "Let's go."

.   .   .   .   .

The view is a painting. The faraway buildings and landscape across the Pacific Ocean all in alignment, and the color is like looking at an enhanced photo. Justin's hand is warm and firm in mine. I take the first step onto the walkaway, and my chest is tight. I don't take the second step.

"It's the perfect ending," Justin squeezes my hand. "Come on."

We walk across the bridge in silence, and I don't look up, just at my feet. Studying in the movements. Pick up foot. Put down. Pick up. Put down.

We have to be close to the other side by now. I stop and look up. Nope. Not at all.

I catch my breath, drop Justin's hand, and lean against the railing of the bridge out across the water. I toy with the locket around my neck. Bubbie bought this to "fit just enough of me to remember", an ash pendant in the shape of a Jewish star.

The view of the far away buildings and landscape makes me feel mid-air, flying. I wrap my arms around myself and shiver. I don't need the ashes to remember.

Justin slides an arm around me. I lean into him and stare across the vast water. We stand like this in silence for a few minutes, the air smelling of ocean and sunshine.

I reach around to unclasp the necklace, but my fingers fumble.

"Let me," Justin says and turns me around. His hands graze my neck as he unlocks the clasp.

"Here," he hands it to me, and the chain curls into the palm of my hand.

I run my thumb along the shape of the star and unlatch the tiny lock. "Good bye, Bubbie." I whisper as the ashes flutter into the wind.

CHAPTER SEVENTEEN
THE (REAL) PERFECT ENDING

The "fasten seatbelts" sign flashes with a ding. Justin holds a greasy paper bag open in front of my nose. "I got some snacks."

Peering in, I see a sugar covered, hole-less...doughnut.

My eyes dart up to his face. "Is this some kind of joke?"

He gives me his *let's get-it-on* smile.

"Are you kidding?" I push the bag away and snatch the Sky magazine from the pocket in front of me. "Jelly doughnuts?"

Out of the corner of my eye, I see Justin's face fall. The bag crumples in his lap. "You don't remember?"

"Remember what?" My stomach growls. "I thought you bought bagels."

He rubs my knee, "You love jelly doughnuts. *Raspberry,* to be specific."

What is he talking about? My stomach makes another grotesque noise.

"Here," he puts the bag in front of my nose again. "You're obviously hungry."

I look at him and then at the bag. The smell of sugar and grease so strong it's almost hypnotic.

Oh. My. God.

Me and Justin on my back porch. *You're obviously hungry. Here.* My stomach growling, me blushing, him handing me a doughnut.

Justin leans into me, the bag crumples a little. "We were in eighth grade. Working on a project for school." His whisper tickles my ear. "I brought the doughnuts. And you...had this interesting way of eating them."

I blush.

"You stuck your finger all the way inside of it and pulled out a glob of jelly." He says into my neck, his lips driving me crazy. "And you licked it from your finger."

The pilot comes on the speaker and says a bunch of things I can't understand. Now Justin is kissing my fingertips.

"And your mouth dropped open," I continue the memory, my free hand brushing the bag that's now between us. "And I said, 'want some?'"

"Then I said, 'Sure' and I sucked the rest of the jelly off your finger." His lips continue to make soft kisses on the palm of my hand while my other one has found its way into the bag and feels around for the powdery soft doughnut inside.

Passengers move around in their seats, a toddler cries, the pilot talks about the weather in New York. The plane begins to roll. My fingers wrap around the plump pastry.

Justin holds my other hand and sits back. "I remember everything, Maddie."

I palm the doughnut and bring it to my lips. We move faster down the runway.

"Like playing air guitar to your dad's seventies rock tapes and kissing you for the first time under that tree."

I take a huge bite and squeeze Justin's hand. "Your right, Justin. I love jelly doughnuts. I really love jelly doughnuts." Then I give him a long and sweet jelly filled kiss.

ABOUT THE AUTHOR

From college essays to resumes to books, as a writing coach, Hannah R. Goodman specializes in helping people find their writer's voice. Her twenty-year career also includes the titles author, teacher, and, more recently, mental health counselor. Among the many titles she has, mother to three girls—two humans and one feline—is most important. Because she spent enough money on them, she wants to share her fancy letters: M.Ed, MFA, and more recently, LMHC.

View other Black Rose Writing titles at www.blackrosewriting.com/books and use promo code **PRINT** to receive a **20% discount** when purchasing.

BLACK ROSE
writing™

CPSIA information can be obtained
at www.ICGtesting.com
Printed in the USA
LVHW04s2034020718
582503LV00003B/655/P